TIM'S HANDS

M. LEE PRESCOTT

Tim's Hands
By M. Lee Prescott

Published by Mt. Hope Press
Copyright 2019, M. Lee Prescott

Cover Image Copyright: eurquhart and Ridofranz
ISBN: 978-0-9982184-9-6

AUTHOR WEBSITE

For my family with love and affection.

CHAPTER 1

"This is beautiful work," Gail Morgan said, running her hand over the surface of the cherry coffee table.

"Thanks," Tim Miller said. "Cherry's a great wood."

Gail held her breath as he ran large, rough hands ran over the smooth tabletop inches from her own. She was there at his workshop, Tim's Hands, to buy a wedding present, but the object of her desire was the man, not the table. Finally, she said, "I don't know Gus and Lynn well, but I'm sure they'll love this. My dad was thinking of buying a matching piece. Have you anything that might work?"

His dark eyes watched her. "Sure, I can find something, or make it. End tables? Maybe a small buffet, or a side table with drawers?"

"Those all sound great. I'll check with him. He might like to come by, or I could bring him?"

After one dance at Gus and Lynn Casey's recent wedding, Gail had been head over heels for Tim Miller, which wasn't at all like her. *I am the steady, sensible Morgan, not some crazed teeny bopper!* She knew the woodworker's reputation. *Every woman in the village—hell every teenager in the village—is in love with the man some call the Heathcliff of Horseshoe Crab Cove. Ridiculous of me to entertain one speck of hope!* Still, like a moth to a flame, she had visited his workshop twice in the past two weeks.

"He's getting married too, I hear."

"Who?" Startled, she realized she had lost the thread of their conversation.

"Your dad."

"Oh yes, that," she said, relieved to find a topic about which she could say something coherent. "My siblings and I are thrilled. It's been twenty years since we lost our mom. We all love Lucy."

"Ms. Brennan's good people. Or does she go by Winthrop now?"

"Yes, she does."

"Her mom's one of the Darn Yarners. Good friend of my mom's."

She nodded. "Yes, the Yarners. Quite a group."

"That's the village for you. It's one huge family, in case you hadn't noticed. Few secrets here. It's a terrific place most of the time unless you happen to be a private person."

"Which you are?"

Surprised, he gave her a sharp look, a glint of fire in the dark eyes.

Gail blanched. "Oh, I'm sorry… I didn't mean to imply. I mean… I don't know you."

He grinned. "No worries. Yes, I'm a private person. Probably why I've chosen jobs where I spend most of my time alone."

"Well, to that end, I'll let you get back to work. I'll chat with my dad and get back to you about the other piece or pieces, but I'm definitely taking the table."

"Now?"

"If it's ready."

"Or I can deliver it to them?"

Gail thought for a minute, afraid to meet those gorgeous eyes again. "Why don't I pay you and leave it here for a day or two? I'd like to get a card to attach to it. Then I'd be grateful if you could deliver it so I don't scratch it. I'll bring the address and the card by."

He smiled, watching her fumble with her purse until she finally extracted a checkbook.

"You do take checks, don't you?" She met his eyes again and nearly swooned. *Get a grip, Gail Morgan! You're not some silly schoolgirl, and besides, he's miles too old for you.*

"Not gonna bounce, is it?"

"No!"

He grinned, throwing up his hands. "Kidding."

"Do I make it out to you or Tim's Hands?"

"Either's fine. All goes into the same bank account."

Her accountant voice almost said, *better watch how you handle your business profits,* but she kept silent, hastily scribbling out the check and handing it to him. "You know you could get double what you're asking for that."

"Maybe."

"I'll be in touch."

"Great."

As she hurried out of the workshop, Gail passed Coop Merrick, the blacksmith who shared the barn with Tim. He called, "Hey," but she barely heard him, so anxious was she to get out to the street where she could breathe. When she stepped outside, she leaned against the rough barn wall, catching her breath, remembering that she needed to speak to Coop about the lamps he was making for her father and Lucy. *Next time,* she thought, *unless I faint dead away the minute I lay eyes on Tim Miller!*

Middle daughter of Richard Morgan, Gail lived with her dad and sister Weezie on the farm and vineyard, Morgan's Fire. Her father's estate lay just outside the village of Horseshoe Crab Cove, or the Cove, as the locals called it. Gail worked for her dad doing publicity for many of his businesses, most recently the vineyard they were endeavoring to bring back to life on the north end of the vast property.

Twenty-six years old, Gail had dated sporadically. One college relationship had been serious, but ended with a broken heart. Hers. She vowed never again, but that was before she met Tim Miller. One glance at the tall, ruggedly handsome woodworker and lobsterman, and lightning struck. Suddenly, dull old Horseshoe Crab Cove seemed a lot more exciting.

She had seen him at her soon-to-be stepmother Lucy's Christmas party, then they had seen each other over New Year's. They hadn't spoken beyond "hello" until they literally ran into each other at the Lab where her sister Ava and husband Dan worked. Tim did occasional jobs for his aunt, Grace Childs Straley, the director. Just in from a run up the river, he was dressed in yellow bib overalls and a red-and-black-plaid flannel shirt. His face was ruddy from the wind and sun, hair drenched, and he carried two buckets filled with seawater and crabs. As Gail rounded the main building, they bumped smack dab into each other. Water and sea creatures sloshed down her front as she screamed, "Oh, oh, oh!"

Her sister Ava flew out of the office. "Wow!" was all she said.

"Wow? How about yuck!" Gail said. "I have a whole day of meetings, and now I smell like dead fish!"

Then she looked up to find the man of her dreams in front of her. *Crash, boom! Lightning!*

A few weeks later, Tim approached her at Gus and Lynn's wedding and extended his hand. "Would you like to dance? I'm not carrying a bucket of water, and there are no fish or crabs in my pocket, promise. Never did get to apologize about that mess because you ran off so fast."

Gail had blushed, then taken his hand. "I guess I might have overreacted just a tad."

Like a fairy tale, he had swept her into his strong arms. "You wouldn't be the first."

She had decided not to wonder what he'd meant by that and enjoy the moment. And enjoy she had. Since then, she'd played Van Morrison's iconic "Into the Mystic" countless times, reliving every second of their dance.

*****

"Hey, buddy," Coop called to Tim as his shop mate carried a pile of wood in from the back. "Village Hardware was robbed last night. That's the fourth or fifth robbery in the past two months. It seems like every year we get a few at this time of year."

Tim shrugged. "Warmer weather brings 'em out. And that's all I'm going to say about this Coop. I'm not starting your guessing game about Izzy," he said, referring to his old girlfriend Isabel Hodges, who had left town ten years earlier a drug addict.

"I'm just saying. It's kind of her M.O. Grab stuff that's easy to sell and run."

"What did I just say? I'm not discussing this. The robberies are probably kids or sleazebags from Bayport."

"Maybe, but whoever this sucks. No one ever locks their doors around here."

"Can't live in a bubble forever," Tim said, absently as he tossed the pile of wood in a barrel.

Coop studied his friend. "Cute redhead, by the way."

"Who?"

"You know who—the beauty who just exited the barn."

"Is it red?"

Coop grinned. "I'd say so. Or auburn?" He watched Tim, whom he'd known since grade school. "You interested?"

"She's buying a table."

"That doesn't mean you can't be interested."

"She's just a kid."

Coop grinned. "Doesn't look like a kid to me."

"Who knows. Certainly not me."

Tim tossed the wood in a growing pile. *Deer in the headlights, more like it and a beautiful one at that.* There was something about Gail Morgan. Ever since he'd dumped water all over her designer suit, he hadn't been able to put her out of his mind. Maybe it was because she was new in town and not one of the silly gaggle of girls that sometimes followed him around. It was embarrassing.

He didn't know much about the Morgans except what he heard around town or his family's dinner table. His sister Karen's best friend was Kyle Morgan's fiancée,

Harriet. Kyle was Gail's first cousin and had moved from his home in Arizona to the Cove to be with Harriet, who taught at Hampton Meeting, a boarding school a short distance from the village. Tim liked the couple. Since Kyle had set up his veterinary practice, he had made a number of house calls to treat their parents' horses, so Kyle and Harriet were often invited to dinner at the farm, sometimes evenings when Tim too was there.

"So you could still ask her out. What's five or six years matter?" Coop called.

"Try ten or fifteen."

"No."

"Doesn't matter. Not interested." *Liar, liar, pants on fire!* He was interested, for the first time since Isabel disappeared.

"She's not coming back, buddy," Coop said for the hundredth time over the last ten years.

"Izzy has nothing to do with it. Now can we drop this, please? I've got a shitload of work to do."

As he began a rough sand of an oak end table, he wondered, as he did every day, *Where the hell is Izzy? Why did she leave? Why hasn't she been in touch? And, at his darkest moments, Is she alive?*

CHAPTER 2

"So do you think you want to purchase a companion piece or not?" Gail asked her father for the tenth time. Their weekly meeting of Morgan Enterprises had just broken up. Her brother Rich had already departed and her sister Weezie was in the kitchen.

"I'd like to take a look at his work first," Richard Morgan said, wondering at the urgency in his daughter's tone. Was it the furniture or the woodworker that accounted for her interest?

Weezie called, "What about me? I'd like to go in on something."

"We'll do it together," he said. "I've been meaning to take a look at Miller's work. The few pieces I've seen around town have been well crafted. Maybe find a few things for this house?"

"Do you want me to set up an appointment?" Gail asked. "It's probably better to do that than just barge in. He has another job, you know."

"Oh?" Richard knew that Tim Miller was the village's most successful lobsterman, but he was mostly interested to hear what his daughter knew about him. This was the most animated and excited he'd seen her since she was a little girl.

"He fishes, for lobsters. And he works part-time for the Lab. Ava and Dan know him," she added, referring to her sister and her husband, who were marine biologists.

"A true jack-of-all-trades or maybe Renaissance man?" he said, a twinkle in his eye.

Weezie popped her head around the door from the kitchen. "Gail has a thing for Tim," she said in a singsong voice.

"Do not!"

Richard smiled, eying his dark-haired youngest daughter. "Don't you have some horses to ride? I'm sure Gus is waiting on you."

Gail rolled her eyes but said nothing.

Richard turned to her. "Honey, why don't you call your Mr. Miller and set something up for this afternoon or tomorrow? I'm pretty free, or I can break free."

"He's not *my* Mr. Miller!" Gail said.

"Ta-ta," Weezie called. "I'm off, but I'm free at those times too. Dying to see the merchandise!"

"I'll call now," Gail said as she stormed from the room.

Richard watched her go and decided he had better make some inquiries about the intriguing Mr. Miller, or the village Heathcliff, as his fiancée, Lucy Winthrop, called him. His nickname for Gail was Mrs. Tiggy-Winkle, after the Beatrix Potter character. His prickly child, she had always reminded him of a hedgehog. He could hear her voice from the front hall, warm, inviting, and friendly, the voice she used when soliciting advertising for one of his businesses. *Hmm*, he thought, *the plot thickens.*

*****

"Who was that?" Coop asked as Tim clicked off from the call.

"Seems we're to have a visit from the Morgan entourage this afternoon."

"That was quick. Gotta go to the hardware store. Be right back."

Yes, it was quick, Tim mused as his barn mate headed out the back door. Gail Morgan was not his type. *Too together.* She was a professional woman, all efficiency and business, but there was a softness there, a vulnerability that one caught glimpses of through the tough façade. That was very appealing. *Watch yourself, buddy,* he thought as the side door opened and the Winthrop sisters stepped in.

"Hey, this is a surprise," he said. His sister Karen's best friend, Harriet Winthrop, was a year younger, her beautiful sister Lucy a few years older. Harriet had been a frequent visitor to the house during high school. He didn't know Harriet or her sister well. A popular, talented athlete, he was always running in and out. His off hours were spent with Izzy.

Lucy smiled at him. "We're actually here to see Coop about my garden arbor."

"Just missed him. He's running to Village Hardware. Shouldn't be long."

"Thanks."

Harriet's eyes scanned the room. "If Kyle and I ever get our own house, I want to commission a dining room table and hutch. You've come a long way since high school shop class, Tim."

He laughed. "I should hope so. My years at the Center are paying off." After Izzy disappeared, Tim had needed to get out of town. With his parents' support, he had enrolled in one, then several more programs at the Center for Furniture Craftsmanship in Rockport, Maine. When he finally returned to Horseshoe Crab Cove, he brought back with him over a dozen exquisite pieces, some of which he sold and others he kept for display. The year he moved back, he had also taken over Rex Miller's lobster fishing license. His father occasionally went out on the boat with him, but mostly he managed the farm and honored his promise to Faith, his wife, that they would take two trips a year, no shorter than two weeks each. So far, the Millers had been to Australia, New Zealand, China, and taken a half dozen trips to the UK and Europe.

As if she could read his mind, Lucy said, "How are your mom and dad? Mom tells me they're in Italy."

"Yup. On a walking tour of Tuscany. They'll be back tomorrow."

"Cool."

"Yeah, they're living the life."

"They're smart. That's the way to do it. Make a pact to take trips every year and stick to it. I'd love to travel more."

"Well, you do have a honeymoon coming up, right?" he said. "I mean, I heard you and Mr. Morgan are getting married."

"Yes," Lucy said, her face lit up in a beautiful smile.

Tim looked from one to the other sister. "What am I saying—you're both getting married, right?"

"That would be correct," Lucy said.

"When are the big days?"

"Ours is very low-key and here next month," Lucy said. "Harriet and Kyle's is next winter in Arizona."

"Still low-key, just farther away, so more orchestration," Harriet said. "It's at Kyle's parents' home in Saguaro Valley."

"They're Gail's aunt and uncle, right?" He realized the moment he spoke that his reference to Gail had come out of left field. *Way to go, man. Nothing like revealing your hand!*

The sisters gave him curious looks as Lucy said, "Yes, Ben and Leonora Morgan. Incredible people, gorgeous ranch."

Tim's face reddened.

Harriet said, "We can wait on the bench out back. It's a beautiful day. We should let you get back to work."

"You're welcome to hang out," he said, "but that bench sounds pretty nice too. Want something to drink? There's water and teas in the fridge."

"Thanks, we're fine," Lucy said as the two women headed for the door.

"What was that?" Lucy whispered as they closed the door behind them.

"I'd say that Tim's more than a little interested in Gail Morgan," Harriet said.

Lucy sighed, sitting down on the bench, closing her eyes, face up to the warm April sun. "How nice for Gail. She needs someone in her life."

"But maybe not Tim Miller," Harriet said. "Not the most grounded person in the world."

"Maybe they'll complement each other?" Lucy patted her sister's hand. "I know I've asked this before, but are you sure you're okay with Richard and me marrying before you two?"

"More than okay. I'm thrilled, and I can't wait!"

CHAPTER 3

"This is quite a shop you have here," Richard Morgan said, wandering around the barn, peering at all Tim's power tools. "I'm very envious."

"Do you have a shop, sir?" Tim followed him, the sisters looking on.

"Small potatoes. Had a bigger one in Maine. I fool around and tinker, but nothing like this. Where'd you learn your craft?"

"The Center for Furniture Craftsmanship in—"

"Rockport. I know it well. Wasn't far from us in Maine. I took a few classes there. Incredible facility. I imagine you went through one of their programs?"

"Three. Took the nine-month intensive, then a couple of specialty courses."

"Well, you learned a thing or two, son. These pieces are truly one of a kind. If I had a place for them, I'd buy every last one."

Tim laughed. "Thanks, but I'd need to keep a few floor models."

Gail cleared her throat. "So, Dad, what do you think? This is the table I got for Gus and Lynn." As she stepped forward, she became intensely aware of the man standing beside her father, sawdust in his dark hair. *Gorgeous, every inch of him.*

"You girls decide. I thought I'd get something from you brother, Weezie, and me, although we four can go in on everything."

"I already bought the table," Gail said. "But if you want, we can give the whole lot between us."

"I love this buffet," Weezie said, running her hands over a maple piece inlaid with strips of cherry and rosewood.

"I thought the end tables were nice." Gail indicated a pair of cherry side tables in the same style as the coffee table.

Richard clapped his hands. "Sounds good to me. We'll take 'em. I'd also like this piece for my office," he added, pointing to a small credenza with three drawers and cabinet doors on either side of it. It appeared to be cherry and had simple inlays of vines along the front.

"You're kidding, right?" Tim said.

"Son, I never kid about what I want. I believe this will be the start of my Tim Miller collection."

"Sir, you didn't even ask the prices."

Richard waved his hand. "I trust you to give me a fair deal. Just tally it up and include the coffee table. You can rip up my daughter's check."

"Dad!" Gail said, voice indignant.

"Let me do this, honey. We can hash out the details later."

Face red as a beet, Gail fished in her purse and pulled out an envelope. "Well, you two better go ahead and sign this, then. One of you can sign for Rich." She threw the card on the table and retreated to the rear of the shop as Tim calculated the final price.

Richard winked at Tim. "You take cards, right?"

"I do," Tim answered, one eye on the angry woman in the corner. The flush of embarrassment only added to her beauty. *Wish I could hug and kiss her all better*, he thought, surprised by his sentiment, which he usually reserved for small children and animals.

Once their transaction was completed and the card signed, they made arrangements for Tim to deliver all three pieces to Gus and Lynn and the credenza to the farm.

"I hear you've got quite an operation going out there with the wild horses," Tim said.

"And thoroughbreds," Weezie said.

"It's a great thing you're doing," Tim said. "My parents were talking about buying one or two of the mustangs once they're trained."

"Yes, I saw your folks at the feed and grain one day. Mickey introduced us." He referred to Mickey Seagal, owner of the farm supply store at the edge of town. Good people.

"That they are. Well, I'll plan to deliver all these tomorrow. Would late afternoon work?"

"Perfect. Then you can stay for dinner, have a tour of the farm. We'd love it, wouldn't we, girls?"

Before Gail could speak, her sister said, "Super! Wait till you see the horses. If you come early enough, you can watch Gus with them. He's pretty incredible."

"I don't want to impose," Tim said.

"Nonsense. We have a fabulous cook and a big table. Join us, please."

Tim nodded. "Thanks, see you tomorrow."

Her cheeks still the color of radishes, Gail gave him a wan smile as she followed the others out. "See ya," she said softly.

Once outside, she strode ahead of her father and sister.

Weezie nudged her father. "Uh-oh, someone's nose is out of joint."

Richard smiled. "She'll get over it." *My little hedgehog is head over heels. That's a new one. Guy's a little rough around the edges, but boy, what talent. Wait till I tell Lucy!*

He knew she was busy with her mother and sister tonight, but he pulled out his phone, rang her number, and left a voicemail inviting her to dinner the next evening. As he and Weezie followed Gail to the Rover, he whistled Simon and Garfunkel's "Feelin' Groovy."

Weezie took his arm. "Dad, you're bad."

"Just happy, baby," he said, squeezing her hand.

CHAPTER 4

"Big date tonight, huh?" Coop asked as he helped Tim load Richard Morgan's credenza into the truck. They had already delivered the Caseys' wedding presents earlier in the day.

"It's a delivery."

"With dinner?"

"Don't start."

"I say go for it, man. She's hot, and her father's loaded."

"I'm going to ignore that. Be careful! You almost hit the side of the truck."

"Wish I was coming. Her sister's hot too."

"And a real spitfire, from what I've seen."

Coop grinned. "Just my type."

"Since when?" Tim hopped into the truck. "Thanks for the help, buddy. See you in the morning."

"Good luck!" Coop called as he watched his friend back out of the lot.

Good luck. I could use some of that, Tim thought, as he drew into the lot behind his apartment. He lived above Village Stationery, two buildings down from Lucy Winthrop's office.

After a quick shower, he dressed and prepared to leave. As he grabbed his keys from the dresser, he gazed at the photo in the silver frame. Izzy, blonde hair blowing in the breeze as she stood on the rocky shore, her slender body in shorts and T-shirt. Waiflike. *Where are you, babe? Just give me a sign you're okay so I can move on.*

It wasn't that he was still in love with Isabel Hodge. He'd let go of that feeling long before she disappeared, but he did feel responsible for her. Some days, the anxiety of not knowing if she was safe or even alive was paralyzing. As he drove out of town toward Morgan's Fire, he wondered if it was time to talk to someone. Time to get past this once and for all.

*****

"Welcome, son!" Richard said, greeting him at the door.

"Hey, Mr. Morgan. I've got your credenza in the truck. Where would you like it?"

"First, there are no Mr. Morgans here. Richard or Dick, that's me. Second, I'll come and help you. I cleared a space in my office so we can carry it right in."

"It's heavy."

"And I'm a farmer. Let's go."

As they walked toward the truck, Gail and Lucy emerged and watched from the porch. Carefully, the two men lifted the piece and headed for the porch. Neither seemed to be straining under the weight.

"Nice to see you, Tim," Lucy said as she held the door open wide.

Gail came to her father's side, nodding at Tim. "Hello."

"Hey," he said softly. *Watch out for those soft hazel eyes and a body that begs to be fucked. Whoa, boy! It's clearly been too long.*

Credenza safely installed, Tim followed his hosts into the family room at the rear of the house. Although large, the room felt warm and inviting with fires blazing in stone fireplaces at either end. Richard waved them to one of several seating areas furnished with a sectional and chairs. This area was nearest to the north fireplace and the dining room. "What can we get you to drink?" he asked.

"The ladies have wine, and I'm having a beer. We have pretty much anything you'd like."

"A beer'd be great, thanks," Tim said as the front door opened and Rich Morgan came in, followed by Ava and Dan Fielding.

"Hi, everyone!" Ava called. "We rode here together. Sorry, Tim, we could've picked you up too."

"That's okay. I had your dad's piece in the truck."

"Oh yes, I want to see it. Hi, Lucy, Gail. Be right back."

Dan nodded hello and followed his wife out of the room. Rich shook Tim's hand, then hugged Lucy. "Good to see you both. If you'll excuse me, I guess I better take a look at the masterpiece, as Dad calls it."

"It *is* a masterpiece!" Richard said, arms around Gail and Lucy. "Where's Weezie, anyway?"

"Right here!" she called from the kitchen. "Someone has to work around here." She came in, jeans and shirt covered with dirt.

"Long day?" Lucy said.

"Something like that. Mustangs kick up a lot of dust. I'm gonna take a quick shower. Be down in a few."

Afraid to look at Gail, Tim turned to his host. "So she's working with the horses?"

"Yup. Thinks she should be in charge, but that's not happening anytime soon. I keep trying to get her to complete her grad studies before she gets too heavily involved, but our Weezie has a mind of her own."

Lucy looked over at Gail, who appeared rooted to the floor, unable to move or speak. "Why don't we all sit?" she said.

Richard raised his beer. "Good idea! See, my beautiful girl is already mistress of the house."

Lucy eyed Gail to gauge her reaction to her father's remark, but she was still frozen, eyes flitting from Tim to the floor. Ava, Dan, and Rich returned, oohing and aahing about the credenza. "Incredible work," Rich said.

"Tim is phenomenally talented," Ava said, turning to her husband. "Isn't he?"

Dan nodded as Rich handed him a beer. "And he's the best lobsterman in the state."

Tim laughed. "Hardly. Can we talk about someone else now? I'd love to hear about the farm."

"That's right," Gail said, suddenly finding her voice. "We promised you a tour."

"Why don't you take him?" her father said. "I've got a couple of things to discuss with Rich, Ava, and Dan. Hurry up now, or your sister'll want to tag along."

Lucy smiled, watching her not so subtle fiancé maneuver Gail and Tim out the door. She said, "And I've got a couple of quick phone calls to make."

CHAPTER 5

"Sorry about that," Gail said. "That would be Dad trying to push us together."

"I'm not sorry," he said as they walked toward the barn.

"It's incredibly embarrassing."

"Well, I'm not much good with crowds. Kind of a hermit, really. I prefer one-on-one."

Gail smiled. "Me too. Maybe it's because we both have big families. Anything for a few minutes of peace and quiet."

"I hear you."

"How many Millers are there?"

"Our immediate family? Six kids. You?"

"Eight."

"Got us beat." He smiled, the smile that made every woman in the village swoon. "This property is amazing."

"Dad knows how to pick 'em. This is the main barn. There are two sections. They originally thought they would have to separate the wild horses from our stable horses, but Gus thinks the mustangs will do better socializing with the others."

"I hear you had a bit of trouble with one of them."

She nodded. "Tornado. Rich and I wanted to get rid of him, but Weezie and Gus prevailed, and they were right. He's coming along. Here's his stall." She made clicking sounds, and suddenly, an enormous head poked out the stall door. Gail jumped back.

"Wow, he's a big one," Tim said, stroking the huge black head.

Unlike her, Tim hadn't flinched, but had stayed still when the horse appeared.

"You're not afraid of horses?" she said.

"Nope. Love 'em."

"I'm afraid, especially of this one."

"Understandable since he kicked your dad in the head."

"Still, I wonder if I'll ever get used to them."

Tim continued to stroke Tornado's nose, the horse softly nickering. "They're amazing creatures. Each with its own personality. Do you ride?"

"Only a couple of times."

"Maybe we should go out sometime? My parents have a couple of real gentle mounts at the farm. I'm a shitty rider, not like my siblings, but I do love the Loop Trail around the coast and village. It's pretty incredible. We're lucky."

"It would have to be a *very* gentle horse to get me out of the corral," she said. "Come on. We can walk to the top of the rise, then head back."

When they reached the crest of the hill, the river flowed in front of them, the peninsula and village to the south and the fields and vineyards to the north.

"Wow, and I thought views from the Point were spectacular. This is amazing."

"Yes." She pointed to her left. "The vineyards are about a half mile that way. The road goes from behind the house. You can just make out the frame of the processing barn Dad's building. It's all a little crazy, if you ask me. They're not even a hundred percent sure the vintner can bring back the vines."

He gazed down at her. "If you build it, they will come? Isn't that the expression? Besides, they can always plant new vines."

"And wait another gazillion years for them to start producing?" *I could get lost in those eyes*, she mused, their dark depths warm as they met hers. "I mean…I don't mean to be negative. My father always teases me for that. He calls me his hedgehog 'cause I'm prickly. It's so embarrassing."

Tim smiled. "Well, for what it's worth, you don't seem at all prickly to me."

Gail blushed crimson, looking away. "That's 'cause you don't know me well enough. Cold fish. Debby Downer, I've heard 'em all, and they fit."

His hand gently cupped her chin, and he turned her to face him. "Hey, don't sell yourself short. You're a beautiful woman. I'd describe you as red hot. Certainly not cold."

"Thank you for saying that, but as I said, when you get to know me, you'll sing a different tune."

"Let's see," he said, leaning in for a kiss.

Just as his lips grazed hers, a cry came from below. "Yoo-hoo!" They turned to spy Weezie at the bottom of the hill. "Hey, guys! Dinner!"

Gail smiled, patting his strong forearm, every fiber of her being aching for the touch he had withdrawn. "That's my sister. Impeccable timing."

He chuckled. "'But there *will* be a time when Weezie Morgan's not around. I promise."

In spite of the heat of the moment, Gail laughed. "You may be seriously crazy, Tim Miller."

"Maybe." As they turned to head back, he noticed the bench. "Beautiful piece," he said, eyeing the seat perfectly situated for viewing the fields to the north.

"That's my mom's," she said as they stood side by side, admiring the ornately carved bench, teak flowers and leaves trailing over its back and down its strong, sturdy legs. A small brass plaque on the front edge of the seat nestled between a cluster of vines read: *Laura Morgan, beloved wife and mother: Cross the meadow and the stream and listen as the peaceful water brings peace upon your soul.*

"It was in Maine, but Dad wanted her with us, so my sister Pam brought her down. She would have liked it here. Can't see the river when you're sitting, but she loved wildflowers, and there's a beautiful stream about three hundred yards down that path. Dad makes sure it's kept mowed."

"I'd love to see it."

"Sometime, but my sister will begin bellowing again if we don't go down. Come on."

She fought a strong urge to take his arm as they descended. *Too forward,* she decided, *and I might faint.*

CHAPTER 6

"So you spend the summer lobstering, do you?" Richard asked as the group dined on salmon, new potatoes, and a crisp spring salad.

"Most days. Still work in the shop at night and some days, depending on whether I have commissions."

"And he works for us," Dan said.

Richard gave his son-in-law a quizzical look. "Oh?"

Ava nodded. "You know I was telling you, Dad? About the poaching of horseshoe crabs in the river?"

"I do recall something about that. Who's doing the poaching and why?"

"Guys in little skiffs set traps, usually before dawn and dusk. They sell the crabs to eel, conch, and whelk fishermen for bait," Tim said.

"All illegal," Dan said. "The state used to set quotas, but the crab population has dwindled so much that there's now a moratorium on any horseshoe crab harvesting."

"A component in their blood is also used to test pharmaceuticals for bacterial contamination," Ava said.

Dan shook his head. "I wish I could say the laws are to protect the crab that's been around since the dinosaurs, but they're mostly trying to conserve the red knot population. Red knots are shore birds that eat horseshoe crab eggs. They're mostly found in the mid-Atlantic. Their numbers are dangerously low."

"Fascinating," Richard said. "Where do you come in, Tim?"

"If on my way in or out, if I see traps, I empty them. A buddy of mine and I sometimes go out at odd times too. We keep track of release numbers."

Gail listened to the conversation, her eyes rarely leaving their handsome guest. Finally, she said, "Horseshoe crabs are one of my favorite creatures."

Tim gave her a surprised look. "Mine too."

Weezie waved her fork. "That's true about Gail. My sister used to go out every spring morning at the crack of dawn to rescue the horseshoe crabs turned over on our beach."

Tim nodded. "Seagulls eating the eggs?"

Gail said, "Yes, horrible creatures."

"Some of that may have been red knots," he said. "There are still some in Maine."

"And not only did she rescue the horseshoe crabs, she'd play school with them in the afternoons. There were always dozens of them in the shallow water. She'd line them up and—"

Gail rolled her eyes. "Exaggerating as usual. I might've done that once or twice, when I was little."

Richard grinned, turning to Tim. "We brought our kids up to appreciate and preserve the natural world. In one way or the other, they've all shown their commitment to that. I'm very proud of them."

Rich had listened quietly to the conversation, saying little thus far, and now nodded at his father's words. "Growing up on Land's End Farm must have instilled the same appreciation in you and your siblings."

"Yup, and some of us are still 'on the farm' in one way or the other," Tim said.

Rich, Ava, and Dan left first to get home for the sitter, then Lucy said good night. As Tim grabbed his jacket, Weezie stood beside him and Gail, clearly intending to walk him to his truck. Then her father intervened. "Come on, Weez. I need you in the office. Gail can walk Tim out. Say your goodbyes. Night, son."

When they stood by his truck, she said, "I'm sorry. My father is beyond embarrassing."

"No worries. He cares about you. You're lucky."

"Yes, although sometimes I'd like to bop him on the head."

"This was fun, thanks." Gentle fingers brushed back a lock of her hair.

"I'm glad you came."

"Me too."

Before Gail knew what was happening, his lips found hers, and he drew her close. The kiss lasted only a few seconds, but it was enough to make her legs wobble and to set her body on fire. When he stepped back, she said, "That was a surprise." She was afraid to breathe.

"I hope not an unwelcome one?"

"Not at all."

"So, want to go out sometime in the real world, just the two of us?"

She smiled. "Without the cast of thousands?"

"Something like that."

"I'd like that."

"I'll give you a call, okay?"

"Yes, good night." She stood on tiptoes and kissed him lightly before stepping back so he could open the truck door. *If he'd asked me to make love right here in the driveway, I'd have said yes!*

As the truck disappeared, she headed for the house on shaky legs. When she stepped into the house, she was whistling.

Her father caught her on the stairs. "He's a great guy."

"What did you do, tie Weezie to your new credenza?"

"No, we had something to discuss."

"Uh-huh. Night, Dad." She hugged him. "You're incorrigible you know."

"Anything for my baby girl. Night, princess."

Gail didn't even bother to chide him for using the childish nickname. She climbed the stairs humming, a huge smile on her face.

CHAPTER 7

"So how'd your date go?" Coop asked, finding Tim sanding a table leg.

"You mean my date with half the Morgan family?"

"So?"

Tim set the sander aside and looked at his friend. "So maybe I'll take her to dinner sometime."

"Great. That's what I like to hear."

"What are you, my mother?"

"No, your buddy who's sick of seeing you moping around."

"I don't mope."

"Yes, you do. And you're alone, even when there are women throwing themselves at you everywhere we go. I wish I had that problem."

Tim grinned, tossing a rag at Coop. "You have plenty who'd be happy to date a beefy, Ron Howard lookalike."

"Ha-ha. Aunt Bee, maybe," he said referring to the character in the *Andy Griffith Show*, which was often on in the background when they hung out at Tim's. Andy Griffith was one of Tim's heroes.

"Or Barney Fife?"

"You like her, don't you?"

That's putting it mildly. Feels like a forest fire on a hot airless day whenever she's around. "She's great, but I wonder what she sees in me. She's an educated professional woman, and I'm a fisherman."

"And the best woodworker in New England, maybe the country."

"Now I know you're delusional."

"Besides, I'll wager you're as educated as she is."

Tim shrugged. His years as a Dartmouth undergraduate were a mixed bag. He loved his studies and the area around campus, hiking the mountains and skiing and snowshoeing all winter, but living in the dorm had been hell until he found a compatible roommate. He'd also missed Izzy, who was at Brown.

After Dartmouth, he had enrolled in the Earth and Environmental Science Masters at Wesleyan, a one-year program that coincided with Izzy's police academy and rookie training. He'd lived in off-campus housing, which had suited him better. Yes, by the classic definition, he was, indeed, educated, but everything had fallen apart when Izzy disappeared. Tim immediately retreated into activities that ensured he was alone. The woodworking courses in Maine had pulled him back into life.

"Can we get back to work now, please?"

"Yup. I've got a delivery to make anyway," Coop said, grabbing two floor lamps. "Want me to bring lunch on my way back?"

"Great. Café?"

Coop nodded.

"Pastrami on rye, chips, and green iced tea. Thanks."

As Coop closed the door, Tim sat, setting aside the hand sander. *Coop is right. It's time to get back into life.*

*****

Gail knocked at the door of Merlin's Closet, Lucy's mail-order children's book business housed on the second floor over Cove Toys and Games.

"Come in," Lucy called.

"I've been sent with a wedding list," Gail said, nodding to her brother Wolfie, a part-time employee of the business Lucy ran with her partner, Lolly LaSalle.

Lucy laughed. "He just called. I've need about five minutes to finish something, then we can head to the café for lunch or tea. Do you mind sitting, browsing? Or feel free to go down and stroll the sidewalk. The weather's glorious."

"Thanks, I'll hover over my brother and browse," she said. "What'cha workin' on, baby brother?"

He gave her a look. "Really?"

"I'm *really* interested. In fact, I'm jealous. This seems like a cool job, surrounded by all these amazing books."

Lucy looked up from her work, reading glasses perched halfway down her nose. "Surrounded may be the key word in this case. Wolfie helps make order out of chaos."

"I'm doing inventory," he said. "We're regrouping after book fair season, gearing up for a few more next month. Then there's school orders for next fall. They're starting to trickle in."

Gail sat beside him, flipping through a copy of *Merci Suárez Changes Gears*. The back cover described a strong, plucky young heroine navigating life in an intergenerational family. "This sounds like a wonderful book."

"It's a Newbery winner," he said.

"I'd love to read it."

"Take it," Lucy said. "My treat."

Gail sat down, back against the wall, and began reading.

Fifteen minutes later, after taking Wolfie's lunch order, the two women strolled down Main Street to the Cove Café. They both ordered kale soup and a half a sandwich, Lucy's chicken salad, Gail's a BLT. The waitress brought waters and iced teas.

Lucy took a sip of tea and gazed over at her companion. "So what are the marching orders for today?"

"Well, let's see. He's given me the final guest list, including whoever he added to your original one. Maybe you can look it over?" Gail handed her two sheets of paper.

"I'm sure it's fine, but let me take a peek." She scanned it quickly. "Looks great. Has he given Mavis the new count, or shall I?"

"He's planning to call his 'dear friend' once he gets the okay from you on the new list."

Lucy gave her a thumbs-up. "I should feel offended that I have so little to do with planning this wedding, but I don't. It's actually very freeing."

Gail chuckled. "He loves it. Besides, he's still complaining about being superfluous on the farm, so this gives him something to do. You know he actually announced at breakfast that he's going to talk to Tim about investing in his business."

"Which one?"

"Woodworking. Dad loves his credenza, and he's already planning to commission a number of other pieces. Wants Tim to publish a catalogue. Poor man won't know what hit him if Dad ever follows through."

Lucy smiled, thinking how nice it was that her relationship with Gail, which had a tough beginning, had now softened into a friendship. She liked all Richard's children, but was especially fond of Gail and Wolfie, the latter who lived in the apartment above her garage. "What are the odds of that?"

"Depends how busy this wedding keeps him."

Their sandwiches arrived, and they chatted about flowers and food, both of which Mavis had arranged. The wedding reception was to be held at Mavis LaSalle's estate, Netherfield Manor, in the Persimmon Room, but two days before, a family barbecue was planned in the farm's largest barn. Initially, Mavis had pooh-poohed the idea, but after Richard gave her carte blanche to transform the space, she had jumped right in. With the barbecue less than a week away, she already had ficus trees lining the walls, twinkle lights everywhere, and five of her signature farmhouse, wrought iron chandeliers hanging from the rafters. Richard had insisted on purchasing them for future events. Tables, chairs, and bright linens and tableware had been ordered. Callie Richardson, Richard's cook and housekeeper, insisted on making the desserts for the barbecue, and she would also be making the wedding cake.

Lucy had wanted to host a rehearsal dinner the following evening at her house, but between the Morgans—east and west—and her family, the numbers necessitated a move to the function room at Ballards, her favorite restaurant just north of the village. "We really know how to fill up a place, between these big families," she said.

Gail nodded. "Especially with the big crew coming from Arizona. I think we finally have places for them all to stay."

Lucy reached across the table and took her hand. "This is really fun doing this with you."

Gail beamed. "I'm enjoying it."

"Well, if I don't say it enough, please know how grateful I am for your help."

"My pleasure."

A mischievous gleam in her eye, Lucy set down her iced tea. "Now, enough about the wedding. Tell me about Tim."

Gail blushed. "There's nothing to tell, so far, at least. He called, and we're having dinner tomorrow night."

"That's good. You like him, don't you? And don't worry, nothing you say will get back to your father. Promise."

"I do, but I understand he has quite the reputation with the ladies."

"Only in their eyes. Women swoon over him, but who wouldn't? As far as I know, he seldom reciprocates."

"Why?"

Lucy smiled. "Hasn't found the right person until now."

"I don't know about that." More blushing. "So he hasn't had girlfriends in the past?"

"Well, yes, he had a very serious girlfriend, Isabel, all through high school, college, and well into their twenties. It was sad, really. I don't know the whole story, but Izzy, as she was called, became a police officer after college. She was part of a regional task force. Quite an important job for a young officer. She did that for a few years, then suddenly she quit, left town, and disappeared. By all accounts, Tim was devastated. He retreated into himself and left behind a promising career.

Finally, he headed to Maine and the woodworking courses. When he came back, he basically changed his life. Took over his father's lobster licenses, started Tim's Hands, and that was that."

"And this Isabel never came back?"

Lucy shook her head. "She had very few ties to the village. Her parents died young, and she was raised by an elderly aunt who died several years ago."

"That is sad. Poor Tim."

Lucy leaned across the table. "Yes, and speaking of Tim, here comes Coop. We'd better change the subject."

"I'll let you get back to work," Gail said. "I've got a meeting about the vineyard at two."

"How's that coming along, anyway?"

"Slowly, but the vines do seem to be viable."

Before she could grab the check, Lucy reached over and said, "This one's on me."

The two women walked out together, saying hello to Coop, who leaned against the takeout counter.

"He's another cutie," Lucy said as they strolled up the sidewalk to Gail's car. "I'm always surprised he doesn't have a girlfriend."

They said their goodbyes, and Gail drove toward home, the story about Tim's past haunting her thoughts.

CHAPTER 8

"This place is great," Gail said as they sipped margaritas, gazing out at the bay. "I'll have to bring the family here. It reminds me of one of our favorite seafood places in Maine."

Tim nodded, his smile warm. "Yeah, I like it. Low-key, great food, and out of the way. You look pretty, by the way. That shirt suits you."

Gail blushed, pleased that she had taken time to carefully select her attire. He'd told her casual, so she dressed in stylish faded denim skinny jeans and a lacy, eyelet blouse with dipped neckline, tonal embroidery, and scalloped, curved hem. It was a more feminine style than she usually favored, and he was right, it did suit her. "Thanks. I'd say you look great too, but I'm not sure that's appropriate." *He'd look amazing in a burlap sack, but the blue work shirt and jeans look pretty gorgeous. Wonder what's underneath them? Oh wanton, shameful woman that I am!*

"What's new over at the Morgan estate?" he asked.

"Everything. The vineyard looks like it's going to produce. My sister Pamela arrives tomorrow, and the mustangs are settling in."

"Where's your sister coming from?"

"Maine. She's moving down, looking for work and staying at the farm. Temporarily, at least."

"What does she do?"

"She's a social worker. Works mostly with adolescents in Maine. She's hoping to consult in the schools, but we'll see. Our family's very close, and it's hard for us to be far apart."

"I hear you. Big families. My siblings are all close by except the oldest. My sister Rachel lives in Chicago."

A slim, dark-haired waitress came to their table. Her name tag said *Kim*. "You folks ready to order?"

They both ordered lobsters, which came with early asparagus and salad. When she disappeared, Gail said, "So you got a good taste of my family the other night— probably way more than you needed. What about your family? Tell me about your life to this point?"

"My family's great. Mom and Dad are hardworking, salt-of-the-earth types. She's a Darn Yarner like Lucy's mom. So are my two aunts, Hope and Grace. Hope runs the yoga studio where your brother's girlfriend works. Have you been there?"

"Ex- girlfriend, I hear and yes, I've taken a bunch of classes from Sara and a couple of other instructors. Your aunt's a great teacher and incredibly flexible for her age."

"Yeah, Hope's pretty incredible." *So are you, Gail Morgan.* Her eyes lit up as she talked, her lovely features enhanced by smiles and laughter. *Not sure if you're ready for this, buddy, but she's sure worth trying.* The curve of her breasts, the round arch of her feminine shoulders, her full, luscious lips. They were enough to send his libido into overdrive, and they'd barely kissed.

Gail set down her drink. "So…what about the rest? Your other siblings? Your path from boy to now?"

For few seconds, Tim eyed her, curious about the reason for all her questions. *Had she heard about Izzy? Was this the third degree?* He definitely wasn't ready for that.

As if sensing a change in his affect, she said, "If I'm being too nosy, I apologize. You can tell me to mind my own business anytime. I love to hear people's stories, but I don't want to pry."

He grinned, the cloud in his eyes gone. "No worries. I'm kind of a loner, hermit, whatever. Not used to opening up about myself, I guess. There's not much to tell. The usual—college, grad school, then I went to Maine for the course I was telling you all about at dinner. Kind of did a U-turn in my life. Still use my education in my work with the Lab. Mostly it's a good balance."

"Ava and Dan say you've been invaluable."

"It's been fun. I like to be out on the water. My lobster pots are in the Bay and a few in open ocean. Much wilder out there. The river flows, you know?"

"Spoken like a true flower child, or son of flower children," she said, raising her glass.

"Yeah, that's me. What about you? What's your path been to now?"

"You mean the one where I haven't left home except for college?"

"So you did go away to school?"

"In Vermont. I went to Middlebury, then got my MBA at Wharton. That was brutal. I loved the courses, but being so far away in Pennsylvania, not so much. Dad was traveling a lot then, and he always tried to stop in. My brother Ben started his first residency in Philadelphia my last semester, so we'd get together sometimes. That helped."

"No man in your life?"

She shook her head. "Not now."

"I'm surprised," he said, his eyes warm as they met hers.

Gail shrugged. "Not very loveable, I guess. That's the feedback I seem to get."

"From who?"

"Men I've dated."

"Well, they're jerks."

She gave him a shy smile. "Maybe. You think they're wrong?"

"Dead wrong."

Kim arrived with lobster bibs, salads, and utensils. "Here you go. Lobsters'll be out soon. Can I get you anything else? Another drink?"

They both ordered beers, and Kim nodded, then moved to her next table.

Gail took a deep breath. "Are you flirting with me?"

He chuckled. "Yes, I guess I am."

She couldn't stop smiling as she ate the crisp, delicious field greens, the dressing a delicate lemon vinaigrette. It had been a while since someone had flirted with her. She liked it.

CHAPTER 9

Tim picked up the check while Gail used the ladies' room. Now he held the door as they exited Bluewater Seafood. "There's a really nice walk along the seawall from here. You interested before we head back?"

"I'd love to."

The seawall followed the coast road. In the growing twilight, streetlights cast soft light on the wall at sporadic intervals as an almost-full moon rose. Waves crashed below them, occasionally sending sea spray their way. "This reminds me of Maine," she said as they strolled side by side, brushing against each other from time to time.

He nodded. "Craggy and wild. I have pots out there about a quarter mile. Real strong riptides here."

"Do you always work alone?"

"Most of the time, but I hire a couple of village kids when it's busy. Easy to find people in the summer months. Not so easy now."

Surprised, she paused. "You go out now?"

"Yup. April to October."

Gail shivered. "Must be cold."

"Not bad. You cold now?"

"No, just thinking about being out there on a little boat, that's all."

He put his arm around her shoulders. "Better?"

"Much," she said, leaning into him, warmed by his nearness.

Shortly after the seawall ended, they came to a small park with a grassy area and a few benches. "Seabring Park," he said. "A gift to the area by our village's very own Darn Yarners."

"You're kidding?"

"Nope. In between all their kibitzing, that group does all kinds of civic projects. They raised close to twenty thousand dollars to fix the wall and create this little contemplative space. That's what they call it." He pointed. "There are plans for a labyrinth over there. They just have to raise a bit more cash. Apparently, they're planning something for May. A fair or something."

"I love labyrinths. I took a workshop about them when I was at Omega a few years ago. It's a retreat center. Do you know it?"

"Heard of it."

"I came back home and begged Dad to build a labyrinth on our Maine property, but then he started making plans to move south. Hey, I'm sure he'd be happy to contribute to this project. He loves stuff like this. And I can help. I'm a pretty good fundraiser."

"I bet you are." He smiled as he watched her gesturing while they sat on a bench, the crashing ocean in front of them. The spot was shielded on the other three sides by brush and wild beach roses, their own private sanctuary as the sun set.

She looked up, and before she could speak, he leaned down and kissed her, gently at first, then more deeply, insistently. He reached round and cupped her cheeks in his rough hands, drawing her closer. Gail responded, turned to him, her arms reaching up, circling strong shoulders. His hand moved downward to her breasts, and she sighed as he stroked and caressed.

"Too much?" he asked, warm eyes finding hers in the moonlight.

Gail shook her head, offering herself to him as he trailed kisses down neck. "God you smell good," he whispered gruffly. "Not sure if I'll be able to stop if we go much further."

"Then don't," she said, stepping up and around, straddling him, her legs through the open back of the bench. She could feel his erection between her legs, awed by its size. She began swiveling her hips, rubbing against him, every part of her screaming to feel that massive bulk inside her, filling her, completing her.

"And you said you were unlovable. What the hell is this?" Tim asked, hands under her shirt now, squeezing, teasing, tweaking her nipples to hardness.

Gail pulled back and stood, unzipping her jeans and letting them, then her panties fall to the ground. Without a word, she straddled him again, the rough fabric of his jeans teasing between her legs, his cock stroking her wet, warmth.

"You sure about this?"

"Do you have a condom?"

"I do."

"Then I'm sure," she said, boldly taking hold of his fly, unzipping and releasing him.

He sheathed himself in one smooth move and pulled her down onto him. "Oh baby, you have no idea," he said as he plunged into her moist, hot depths.

Gail smiled, arching her back, opening herself, receiving him, echoing his every move with her own insistent longing. "I think I do." That was the last coherent thought she had as they took each other over the moon to a blinding, crashing climax. When her orgasm released her, Gail fell against his chest, spent, her legs shaking. Tim wrapped his strong arms around her, and she rested, the cool ocean breeze at her back.

As the fiery glow of their lovemaking ebbed away, she felt a chill run through her. As if a switch flicked on, she sat up. "Oh, what have I done? I've never... I can't. I've got to go."

She pulled back. As he slipped out of her, she stood, searching for her clothes, her legs still trembling.

Tim reached out, taking her arm. "Hey, what's going on? You okay?"

"No… Yes… I don't know. I've got to go. Now! What were we thinking? What if someone had happened along?" She pulled on panties and jeans, slipping into her shoes that had been cast aside.

Tim stood, zipped up, then gently grasped her shoulders. "Gail, what is it? What's wrong?"

Tears streaked her beautiful face. "Can we just start walking? I'll feel better if we start back."

As they walked in silence, her breathing slowly returned to normal. When they reached his truck, she ran around and hopped in without a word. He got in, slipped the key in the ignition, then turned to her. "Talk to me, please."

"I'm sorry," she said, calmer now. "I've just never experienced anything like that. It just threw me. I… I… I don't even know what to say. It was like I was split apart and thrown out of myself. I was totally lost, gone."

He reached across and took her hand. "That's a good thing, isn't it?"

"I haven't the faintest idea. It scared me."

"What about other guys? I mean you're not… This wasn't your first time, was it?"

"No, but I can tell you right now, sex has never been like that. I mean I don't have a lot of experience. And, in case you haven't noticed, I like to be in control. That was totally out of control."

"Out of control great, from my perspective."

"Well, that's you. You're much more experienced."

"And older?"

"That too."

"If it makes you feel any better, I've never experienced that kind of intensity with another woman."

"Is that a good thing, do you think?"

He chuckled. "Yes, it's a great thing. Now let's get you home. You're shivering. Here, take my jacket." He shrugged out of his oilskin jacket and wrapped it around her shoulders.

They said little on the drive back. When they reached the farm, he parked and came around to open her door. "Can I kiss you good night?"

"Just a hug, if that's okay?"

He wrapped strong arms around her, drawing her close, kissing the top of her head. "Good night, sweet Gail, the most lovable woman I know."

"Night," she said, handing him his jacket as she stepped back, then almost ran to the porch steps.

She closed the door and leaned back against it, saying a silent prayer of thanks that her father and sister were out. Still shaken, she headed upstairs. Her legs felt like wet noodles, and she fought the urge to burst into tears. *What is wrong with me? Do I want to cry 'cause I'm happy or devastated or something else altogether?* No answer came as she fell asleep, a dream-filled, restless sleep.

*****

Tim threw his keys on kitchen counter and grabbed a beer. He didn't make a habit of drinking late at night, but this one had been a doozy. One minute, he was as close as he could get to a beautiful woman, and the next, she was running away like he was the black plague. *What the heck was that?* He sat on the couch and flipped channels for a while, then chugged the beer and headed for bed. After washing up, he paused at the photo of Izzy and him smiling at the camera. As he did every night, he said, "Where the hell are you, babe?"

CHAPTER 10

Pam arrived at Morgan's Fire midmorning, a small moving truck with her. Most of her belongings were stored in the smaller barn, and her sisters helped her bring boxes and suitcases to her second-floor bedroom. "Why don't you just stay here permanently?" Weezie asked as she and Gail watched her unpack.

Pam looked up from her unpacking. Her strawberry-blonde hair was tied back in a sloppy ponytail, and she blew errant locks from her forehead. She smiled, her pale blue eyes twinkling. "You know I love you guys dearly, but I need my own space."

"And there's plenty of it here," Weezie persisted, flopping down on a deep upholstered chair.

"Maybe, but let's enjoy it while we can. I'm going to use the next month to find a place, look for a job, and settle in."

"Well, we're glad you're here," Gail said.

"You're awfully quiet today," Pam said, eyeing her auburn-haired sister.

"Not much to say except hurry up and unpack so you can help with the wedding."

"Gail's got a boyfriend," Weezie said in a singsong voice.

"Oh?"

Gail blushed, and her eyes darted around the room. "One date."

Pam studied her for a few seconds before saying, "So what about the wedding anyway? What has to be done? Dad told me some fancy wedding-planner friend was doing it all."

Gail's face brightened, as she was clearly relieved to be off the subject of boyfriends. "Yes, Mavis LaSalle's doing most of it, but there are still a million details. Lucy and I have been meeting nearly every day."

Pam sat beside her on the edge of the bed. "You've warmed to Lucy, haven't you?"

Gail nodded. "Yes, I was an asshole. She's terrific and really good for Dad. He's so happy. For the first time in twenty years, he seems grounded and at peace. It's like after Mom died, he turned into a ping-pong ball and has spent all these years bouncing around from place to place, project to project just so he doesn't have to deal with the loss. Now, with Lucy, he can stop. He's a different person, isn't he, Weez?"

"Ditto. I never knew Dad with Mom, but I agree, he's a new man. Loves the farm and is very involved. He's also happy to let it go and let everyone else take charge. Can you imagine Dad doing that ten years ago?"

Pam laughed. "Never. Where is the man of the hour this morning, anyway?"

Weezie hopped up. "Down at the vineyard with Wolfie and the vintner, which reminds me, I gotta go. I promised to grab lunch for everyone 'cause it's Callie's day off."

As the sound of Weezie's steps receded, Pam leaned back and turned to her sister. "Okay, what's going on?"

"Nothing," Gail said, eyes filling with tears.

"That doesn't look like nothing. Come on, we redheads have never had secrets."

"It's not a secret. I'm just confused and kind of frantic."

"About?"

"About falling for someone who could break my heart, not to mention a host of other fears. He has some kind of lost love, I'm a control freak, I barely know him and yet had wild, unbridled sex last night."

"Ooh, unbridled sex—that sounds very promising," Pam said, reaching over to pat her hand.

"Well, it isn't. It's alarming and totally out of character for me."

"Maybe that's a good thing?"

"Never mind shrinking me."

Pam smiled. "I'm not a psychiatrist."

"You know what I mean. I can hear your social worker voice loud and clear."

"This is my sister voice, dearie. I'm talking to my sister who I love very much and who is obviously struggling with something. Conflict? Fear? Love?"

"Who knows, all of the above."

"Tell me about him."

"His name's Tim Miller. Comes from a big town family. Parents own Land's End Farm. Remember when we rode out there a few months ago?"

"I do. Is that what he is, a farmer?"

"No, he's a woodworker and lobster fisherman. Dad has one of his pieces in the office downstairs. He's incredibly talented."

"And good-looking?"

"Gorgeous. Apparently, according to Lucy, they call him the village Heathcliff."

"Tall, dark, handsome, and wild?"

"Something like that. He's great, he really is. I'm just scared."

"One step at a time, sweetie. Now what do you say we take a walk? How far is this vineyard?"

"'Bout a half mile."

"Then let's get jackets and go say hi to Dad."

CHAPTER 11

"What's up bro?" Karen Miller asked, spying Tim at the hardware store. "Mom and Dad were just saying they've barely seen you since they got back."

"Been busy," he said, hugging his sister.

"Doing?"

"Everything from furniture to pots. I've been on the river almost every day this week. It's the season."

"Of the bastards who slaughter the crabs?"

"Yup. What's up with you?"

"The usual. Lots of lessons, spring 4-H, and Saturday pony camps. I can always use the help. Hint, hint."

"Didn't I just say I'm busy?"

"And I hear you have a girlfriend? 'Bout time."

He shrugged. "That's debatable."

"What, the girlfriend or about time?"

He grinned. "Both."

"Care to share?"

"Not in the middle of Village Hardware."

"How 'bout lunch?"

"No can do. I'll catch up with you soon, though."

"You better. See ya." Karen waved over her shoulder as she headed for the exit.

*****

When Gail and Pam returned from their walk, Gail found a voicemail from Tim asking how she was. She texted back, *Doing fine. Sorry for my bizarre behavior. Love to talk soon.*

Almost immediately he texted back, *How about a boat ride? Lab dock at 8 am tomorrow?*

Gail replied, *Yes.*

He wrote, *Great. See you then. Dress warm.*

She spent the rest of the day with Pam, helping her sort through things and talking about life and the wedding. Tomorrow, their brothers Teddy and Ben arrived, as well as the Arizona cousins. From then on, life would be bedlam until after wedding weekend.

At dinner, their father said, "Now I hope all our ducks are in a row as far as accommodations."

Gail gave him a look. "All set, as I've told you at least fifty times. Uncle Ben and Aunt Leonora are in one of Mavis's cottages, and Ben, Maggie, and their kids are in the other one with Sam and Rose. Lang, Beth, and Lily, and Robbie and Hope, are at Blueberry Lane B and B, and Spark Foster's at Lucy's mom's."

"Do they have a thing going?" Pam asked, referring to the billionaire college friend of Richard's older brother, who had moved permanently to Saguaro Valley several years earlier. Spark had met Helen Winthrop, Lucy's mom, on one of her trips out West, and they had become good friends.

"Just friends," Richard said. "He comes east, she goes west, but I don't think the twain shall ever meet."

"Lucky thing you decided on a small wedding," Weezie said, pointing a breadstick at her father. "Just the family alone fills up every available space in town, not to mention a huge function room."

"Be great to have so many of 'em here," he said. "Wish Ruthie and her wrangler could make it."

"Harley and she are holding down the fort at all locations. Someone has to be at the stables and farm."

"Still, would've been fun to have every single Morgan together under one roof."

"Well, you're about to get your wish, Dad," his son Rich said, stepping in from the kitchen with a plate of food. "Just got a call from your brother. The Langdons are coming. Ben Senior says they can squeeze Harley, Ruthie, and the baby in with them at the cottage."

Richard clapped his hands. "Terrific! Now let's remember to have Mavis's fancy photographer get a shot of all of us. How many is that?"

"If you include Spark, I believe the number you're seeking is thirty."

"Well, of course we include Spark! Thirty, think of that!" Richard grinned, eyes scanning the table. When they came to rest on Gail, he winked. "And this gal has done yeoman's work pulling it all together."

"Is Lucy's side going to be overwhelmed by so many Morgans?" Pam asked.

Gail shook her head. "I don't think so. Her number is around fifteen. She wanted the whole Darn Yarner group because they're like aunts to her and her sisters."

"What about your guy, sweetie?" her father asked. "Did you invite him?"

"No."

Richard eyed her. "Well, you should. His parents are invited since she's one of the Yarners. Besides, we're havin' a top-notch band, so you'll all need dancing partners. Invite your Mr. Miller and that blacksmith buddy of his. Love to have 'em."

"Coop?"

"Yeah, that's the fellow."

"Well, why don't we go ahead and invite the whole town?" Gail said, setting down her napkin. "Excuse me, I've got work to do!"

"Wait a sec, honey," he called, but Gail was already out the door and halfway up the stairs.

Richard gazed around the table. "What'd I say? Does she have a beef with the blacksmith?"

Weezie leaned toward him and whispered, "More like trouble in paradise, I'm guessing."

"With young Miller? What happened?"

Pam gave Weezie a sharp look. "It's none of our business and should not be a subject for conjecture."

"But—" Weezie said.

"Drop it," Pam said as Rich and their father exchanged looks.

Richard turned to his son. "So, how's the empire doing? We haven't touched base since Monday."

Rich chuckled. "As you well know, the empire is doing just fine. The outlay for the vineyard is setting us back, but we can afford it."

"I should hope so. What about the horses? Weezie?"

"Gus is amazing. You should see the progress he's making with Tornado. One of the others, Piccolo, even let him put a saddle on her."

"To ride?" Pam asked, eyes wide.

"No, but she accepted it pretty well. Gus thinks she might make a good stable horse if we ever get to the point of giving lessons. She's short, steady, and compact."

"That's not really our mission," Rich said. "We're a rescue organization with an aim to build a small thoroughbred stable down the line. As far as Piccolo and Tornado are concerned, you need to think adoption, 'cause that's the end goal."

Weezie sniffed. "Maybe. Time will tell."

Rich narrowed his eyes, gazing from father to sister. "Time will *not* tell. We received all kinds of grant funding for the mustang program, and we can't just up and keep all these horses. Dad, tell her. You've got Crackers and Sheba. Period. Those are the only horses that are staying long-term."

"Your brother's right, baby. Now, I've gotta excuse myself and go call my girl."

Instead of going to his office, Richard climbed the stairs and knocked on Gail's bedroom door. "Hey, baby."

"Go away. I'm fine, Dad. I just want to be alone."

He tried the handle, and the door gave way. When he opened it, he found her curled up on the bed. Richard came to sit beside her, patting her shoulder. "Hey, sweetie, I'm sorry. I really put my foot in it, didn't I?"

"You didn't do anything," she said, voice muffled under a pillow.

"Well, maybe I can help?"

Gail sat up, brushing hair from her red, blotchy face. "I sincerely doubt that."

"Well, I am a man. I might be able to give that perspective."

Despite her distress, Gail smiled. "I see. Did you just beam in from Mars?"

He grinned. "Sure did. Now let's talk this out and find a solution."

Gail reached out, and he drew her into his arms. "Oh, Dad, you always say that. We should have a plaque made for your office that says *let's talk this out and find a solution.*"

"Usually works for me,' he said, patting her back.

"I like Tim. I really do, but I think I jumped in too deep, too fast, and I don't know how to jump out again."

"You know, I don't think Lucy would mind if I told you this, but she felt the same way with me. Different people, different reasons, but same feeling. That jumping into the deep end before you learn to dog paddle in the shallows."

"Exactly."

"Trouble is, affairs of the heart don't always work that way. We meet someone, and it's instant. We fall for them like a ton of bricks. That's how it was with me and your mom, and that's how it was with Lucy. Can't control it. It just happens."

"That's just it. I'm always in control. That's how I function."

He chuckled. "Well, hold on to your hat, baby girl, because when you fall for someone hard, control goes right out the window."

Gail shook her head. "I don't think I can handle that."

"My advice? Don't run away. He's a great guy."

"Yes, he is."

"He isn't pressuring you in any way, is he?"

"No, of course not."

"Then maybe take a few steps back. Be friends. Keep seeing each other and see where it leads. Invite him to the wedding. It's gonna be a fun day. You'll have all your family and friends around. Keep it light."

"Maybe," she said. "He's taking me out on the boat in the morning."

Her father grinned. "Perfect activity for two friends."

"Thanks, Dad."

"No problem. Parents aren't happy when they're kids aren't, no matter what age those kids are. If I don't see you in the morning, have fun on the boat." He kissed the top of her head and left her.

As she washed up, Gail felt calmer. *Friendly boat ride. Let's see how that works when every fiber of my body screams for him.*

CHAPTER 12

Gail parked beside her brother-in-law Dan's truck in the dirt lot behind Cove Lab. As she walked around the building toward the docks, Grace Straley, director of the Lab pulled in. Gail knew Grace slightly from her occasional visits to see Ava. As the tall woman slid out of her battered truck, Gail waved.

"Morning!" Grace called. "You here to see your sister?"

Gail shielded her eyes, waiting as Grace approached. "I'm actually going out on the boat with your nephew."

"Really?"

Gail smiled. "Really."

"That's a first. Where is the boy, anyway?"

"Not sure. I just got here."

Instead of taking the direct route into Grace's office, Grace circled the building alongside her. Dressed in baggy jeans and a bright windbreaker with the logo for Cove Lab and Fisheries, Grace was a handsome woman with sharp angular features and piercing blue eyes. The lab shared the building and docks with Cove Fishery. Belle and Will Pollart ran the docks and fishery. Both Belle and Grace were members of the Darn Yarners, that ubiquitous group of women to which Lucy's mom belonged.

As they rounded the corner of the building, Gail spied Tim on his boat, which appeared to be about thirty feet with a small cabin at the front. The name emblazoned on the back was *Isabel. The mysterious woman in Tim Miller's life.* The boat looked freshly painted, a dark navy with white trim. Tim looked up and waved. "Hey, morning!" In jeans, flannel shirt, faded blue baseball cap, and work boots, he had already discarded his oilskin jacket.

"Morning yourself, nephew. I hear you're taking this pretty lady out for a spin."

"That's the plan," he said. "You want to come?"

"I would, but duty calls. Besides, I'm certain I'd be a third wheel. You're not working out there this morning, are you?"

"No."

"Good, because one of our boats had a bit of trouble down the coast. As these vermin reap greater profits for their thievery, they've gotten more aggressive. Tried to scuttle a boat."

"Not this one and not today," Tim said, coming beside the dock and extending his hand to Gail. "You ready?"

"Not if we might get scuttled out there."

"Don't listen to her. She's getting senile or at least paranoid."

Grace shook her head. "My sister would never forgive me, and I'm pretty certain Gail's dad would have the noose ready. Have a good cruise."

Gail hopped aboard and took a seat in the back. "This really is a small town, isn't it?"

"Very, and getting smaller every minute. No secrets here. That's why I keep a low profile."

The river was glassy as he steered the boat out into the channel, the cries of gulls and osprey heralding their passage. Gail sighed, leaning back with the warm sun on her face. "This is heaven. Thanks for inviting me."

"My pleasure. Mornings are the best. I usually go out at five or six but didn't think you'd want to get up that early."

Gail smiled. "You'd be surprised how much I get accomplished between five and six am. This is a great boat, by the way."

"I like it. Bought it used. It was a lot of work restoring it, but it was worth it. I like wooden boats."

"Pretty name," she said, instantly regretting her words as his expression clouded.

"Yeah…you've probably heard about my… About Izzy."

Gail considered lying, but then decided against it. "Just a little. Your girlfriend, right?"

He nodded. "Ex-girlfriend. I actually bought the boat and named her after Izzy left. I guess I was hoping she might return and I could surprise her. Now, after all these years, I'm just too lazy to change it."

"So you don't hear from her?"

"Nope."

"What happened, if you don't mind my asking?"

"We broke up, she left. Period, end of story."

A deafening silence fell over them as he headed downstream. Every so often, Tim paused to pull a trap, checking for horseshoe crabs. If any were trapped, he released them, discarded the bait, and threw the trap back overboard. She wanted to ask him about what he was doing but couldn't screw up the courage to speak. Why had she mentioned the boat's name? *Stupid, stupid, stupid!*

As they rounded the peninsula, she said, "I'm sorry. I didn't mean to pry."

"No worries," he said, but continued his work as if she wasn't there.

Finally, she decided enough was enough. "Listen, Tim, I obviously struck a nerve back there, and now you're probably wishing I was a million miles away. Why don't you drop me on the shore near the road and I can walk back or call someone to come and collect me?"

Back to her, he stood gazing out at the open bay.

"Tim? Did you hear me? Tim?"

At last he turned to face her. "Yeah, I heard you, and I'm an asshole. You have nothing to be sorry about. I'm so used to not talking about things, especially Izzy, that it's hard to know where to begin.""You absolutely do not have to talk about it. I'm too nosy for my own good."

"Let me drop anchor."

Tim cut the boat's engine and threw the anchor overboard.

Chapter 13

A hundred yards from shore, they were in an inlet surrounded by the tall marsh grasses that grew on the sandy shoreline. There wasn't a house in sight. Great blue herons and egrets waded in the shallows, and an osprey circled overhead.

"What is this place?" she asked, marveling at the quiet enveloping them.

"Brady's Marsh. Cool, huh?"

"Very."

"It's one of my favorite places. All conservation land. Audubon monitors the nesting platforms. We've got lots of ospreys and even a few eagles."

"It's beautiful."

He smiled. "And so are you. How about coffee? I have a thermos. Or I have water."

"Coffee'd be great thanks."

"How do you take it?"

"Black."

He grinned, pouring the steaming coffee into a large, insulated cup. "That's a relief, because that's all I've got."

She accepted the cup, sipping carefully. Grateful for the warmth, she sat quietly, waiting for him to speak.

"So you've heard about Izzy through the village gossip mill?"

"Only that she was your girlfriend and that she left."

He nodded. "We were together all through high school and college. I was in New Hampshire and she was in Massachusetts, but we managed to get together almost every weekend in one of our dorms. We kind of drove our roommates crazy. Senior year, she got an apartment near campus, so that meant I would hightail it out of Hanover every Friday afternoon, sometimes earlier if I could get away.

"Hanover? You went to Dartmouth, then?"

"Guilty."

"Two of my siblings were there, Ava and Rich."

"Yeah, Ava and I compare notes sometimes. I went to grad school after Dartmouth. Izzy came down and lived in Connecticut with me, but she was really unhappy. She couldn't figure out what she wanted to do so she finally came home to her aunt's here in the village. A couple of her cousins are cops, and one convinced her to apply to the academy, which she did. She loved it and did really well.

"We still saw each other whenever we could. After I finished my master's, I came home. By then, she had been recruited to a regional task force, which was kind of a big deal for someone so young. They wanted her for undercover work that guys with families didn't want to do. She was really psyched, but I was leery. The hours were long, and they had her doing some pretty scary shit, excuse my language. That's when she started to change. She'd be gone weekends and three or four days at a time.

"We were living in my apartment, and I worried about her constantly. Then her unit targeted a local gang, drugs and prostitution. She went undercover, and within a month, she was addicted to heroin. I tried everything to get her out, but she was gone. There'd be weeks when I wouldn't hear from her. I went to the regional office and begged them to tell me where she was, but they wouldn't or couldn't.

"Finally, she came home totally messed up, and I gave her an ultimatum. Quit or we were done. She promised she would. The next day, I kissed her goodbye, she left for work, and I never saw her again. No calls, letters, nothing. I went back to her office, and they said she'd disappeared and wasn't working for them anymore."

"How awful for you."

"It was a nightmare. After a year of searching for her, I gave up and went to Maine, to woodworking school. Changed my life and tried to move forward."

Gail glimpsed the pain reflected in his dark eyes and said softly, "I'm so sorry. How long ago was that?"

"Ten years. I'm a lot older than you babe. Thirty six to be exact."

"Not that much older," she said, smiling. "So sad for you and Izzy."

He nodded. "By the time she left, she was stealing from her aunt, Coop, and me. She ripped her aunt's television right off the wall, stole Coop's cash box, my laptop, all the money we had in the apartment. It was a nightmare that I'm sure contributed big-time to her Aunt May's decline."

Gail set down her cup and took his hand.

"No one else knows about the drugs or the stealing. Only Coop, and I'd like to keep it that way."

"Of course. Thank you for trusting me."

"I'm sure if it was warmer, you'd be diving off this boat and swimming like hell to shore."

"No I wouldn't."

"I wouldn't blame you either. Guess it's about time I renamed my boat, huh?" He grinned, and his face began to relax.

Gail leaned over and kissed him softly.

"You know, if you start, it might rock the boat."

CHAPTER 14

Gail wrapped her arms around his broad shoulders and slipped over to straddle him. "This seems like a sturdy old tug."

"I'm not sure, babe. Is this a good idea, after what I just told you? Don't you need time to digest?"

Gail smiled, hand caressing his cheek. "Probably. I was going to suggest that we keep this a friendship. The other night's intensity kind of freaked me out."

"And?" he asked, hands moving up and down her sides, fingers grazing her breasts.

"Then I looked into those big brown eyes and realized that no man has ever made me feel like that. Seems pretty stupid to walk away from that, don't you think?"

He gave her a mischievous look, hands now cupping her breasts, squeezing, massaging. "Hard to put out the fire once it's lit?"

"Something like that."

His lips captured hers with lots of tongue. Gail moved up and down against him, an exquisite frisson of sensation coursing through her as she felt him harden. Afraid to breathe, she arched her back, opening herself to him as he trailed kisses down her neck, hands inside her sweatshirt now, caressing her soft naked breasts.

"Is this really private?" she asked, breathlessly.

"Better be."

Gail pulled back and stood, scanning the shoreline as she slipped off sneakers, jeans, and panties. "Good." She gave him a devilish look and hopped back into his lap.

In the blink of an eye, his fly was down and a condom in place. His fingers slipped between her legs. "Geez, you're wet, aren't you?"

"Waiting for you."

His cock replaced fingers as Tim slid inside her. "Man, you're something, Gail Morgan." She arched her back, urging him to go deeper with each thrust. He grasped her smooth, round ass, trying to hold on as she rose and fell, taking him deeper and deeper. Lost in a miasma of feeling, they moved together to an explosive climax

As her orgasm let down, Gail fell limp, holding Tim's shoulders. "Oh my, oh my," she murmured, kissing his neck.

"Oh my doesn't even begin to describe it, babe."

A sound startled them, and Gail gazed over his shoulder. A boat was rounding the Point and heading parallel them, two men standing in the back, one at the wheel. "Shit," he muttered, turning to shield her half-naked body. "You dress behind me. I've gotta move. I've been trying to catch these guys in the act for weeks."

Gail stooped under the roof of the small open cabin and pulled on panties and jeans. Tim zipped up and hurried to pull the anchor. The other boat was headed south and seemed to be paying them no mind. As *Isabel's* motor roared to life, the men spied them and sped up.

She looked ahead, then at Tim. "What are you doing? Do you have authority to do anything to them?"

"Nope. I just want to get their license number. Can you read it?"

As she squinted, endeavoring to make out the number plate on the side of the boat, one of the men threw a tarp over it. They opened the throttle, and the small light craft sped off, leaving a wide wake.

Tim slammed his fist on the railing. "Bastards. No way we can catch them." He took a few photos with his phone and then turned his boat toward the docks.

"Too bad I didn't think to take pictures first. Could've blown them up to read the license number.

"What do you do with it?"

"The Lab gets in touch with the Coast Guard and local police. We still have to catch them with the crabs, but we can find out where they dock and be waiting when they return to shore."

They said little as they cruised back upriver, giving her time to think about the last hour. It was almost as if she had no control when he was near. *All I need is to catch a glimpse of him and I'm on fire.* She had a sneaking suspicion he felt the same. *Yikes, I'm out of my depth here.*

After tying up, Tim walked her to her car. When they reached it, Gail threw her things in and turned to gaze up at him. He swept her into his arms for a soft kiss. "Thanks for coming out with me."

"Thank you. It was… It was amazing."

"That too."

"Are you free tonight? There's a barbecue at the farm. Real casual. Family and friends."

"Sounds fun."

"Then you'll come?"

"Yup."

Gail smiled. "And, I wanted to ask… I mean, it's Dad's wedding Saturday, and I get to bring a date. Would you like to come?"

"Wow, planning two dates at once."

She blushed. "Is it too much?"

He kissed her forehead. "Not at all."

"If my family is too much tonight, you can always rescind the Saturday invite."

"I come from a big family, remember? I have nerves of steel. What time tonight?"

"Six thirty."

"I'll be there."

CHAPTER 15

Gail and Tim stood just outside the barn, her brothers Ben and Teddy at their side. "You sure you're ready for this?" Gail asked, gazing up at him.

They'd been chatting with her brothers since Tim arrived. Lucy's family was outnumbered two to one by Morgans, and they just kept coming. The air was thick with hickory smoke from three long barbecue grills set twenty feet from the barn.

"Hey, kids." A tall balding man who bore a remarkable resemblance to the actor and politician Fred Thompson clapped Tim on the shoulder. "You must be Dick's kids. I see a family resemblance. Spark Foster, friend of his," he said, pointing to a tall silver-haired man, his arm around a petite blonde.

"Great to meet you," Tim said, extending his hand. "Tim Miller, the only non-Morgan in the group."

"Hi Mr. Foster," Gail said. "Welcome, I'm Gail, and these are my brothers, Teddy and Ben. So great to finally meet you. We've heard so much about you and the Valley."

She reached out her hand, which he ignored as he grabbed her in a bear hug. "No Mr. Fosters here, darlin'. Spark'll do just fine." He greeted her brothers in the same fashion. "I'm the honorary family member. Ben's my lifelong buddy. When my wife died, I came to visit Ben and Nora and basically never left."

Ben and Leonora Morgan soon joined them, hellos all around, and Tim and Gail were swallowed up in the crowd. She held his hand and introduced him as best she could. Grounded and calm, he actually seemed to be enjoying the hubbub. When they bumped into Richard and Lucy, he hugged them both.

"So glad you could come, son," Richard said. "Have you met everyone yet?"

"Getting there, sir. Thanks for having me."

Arm around Lucy, Richard beamed. "Delighted."

Lucy nodded, patting his arm. "And we're so pleased you'll be joining us Saturday."

As they strolled off, Tim said, "Your dad seems really happy."

"He is. Happiest I'm ever seen him. I was pretty young when our mom died, so I don't remember him with her."

"He's a great guy, your dad."

"Yes, he is." She slipped her arm through his. "Let's get a drink, okay?"

Four long tables covered in brightly colored oilskin tablecloths lined the center of the barn, both the front and back doors open to the evening breezes. Gail and Tim sat with her cousin Ben Morgan and his wife Maggie, Ben's brother Sam and his wife, Rose, and Gail's siblings Rich, Teddy, and Ben.

Maggie Morgan turned to them and said, "Poor Tim, this is a lot of Morgans in one place, isn't it? I thought I was outnumbered in the Valley."

"I'm fine. Enjoying myself, thanks," Tim said.

"After hearing about all of you, it's wonderful to have everyone here," Gail said. Tim's knee touched hers under the table, sending a warm shiver through her.

Ben Morgan put his arm around his beautiful wife. "Sure is. Only problem is all these Bens. We've got two at this table and two more roaming around. At least my dad gets called Grandpa and our little fella is Bennie, but now two of us of the same generation are named Ben. Gonna be crazy."

"Yes, but you're miles older than East Coast Ben," Maggie said, winking at Gail's brother. "We could almost call you Grandpa."

Her husband rolled his eyes, squeezing her shoulders. "Pay no attention to her. Been kicked by too many horses. Although I do admit to being a whole lot stupider than my cousin the doctor."

"Hardly," Gail's brother Ben answered. "You're a Stanford grad, are you not?"

"They have to let a few of us 'happy Bs' in to make the others look good."

Maggie laughed. "You'll learn quickly to take very little of what my husband says seriously. Your stables are incredible, by the way."

Rich nodded. "Gus and his crew are doing a great job, and you can thank Sam for the physical spaces. He designed them all, including this barn."

"Which looks suspiciously like Spark's," Ben said, eyeing his brother mischievously.

Gail watched the interplay between the drop-dead-gorgeous Morgan brothers. *Weezie wasn't kidding*, she thought, remembering her sister's gushing about how handsome their cousins were. Her own brothers and the man sitting beside her were no slouches, but there was something about the West Coast crew. Valley sun? And hands down, Maggie was one of the most beautiful women she'd ever met, with her long, luscious dark hair, blue eyes, and curvaceous figure. When they had walked in, every man's eyes were riveted on her.

Tim seemed comfortable and chatted easily with her brothers and Rose Morgan, who sat to his right. For most of the meal, he held Gail's hand under the table, fingers gently caressing her palm. Rather than a distraction, she found his touch calming.

"Did you all come on Spark's plane?" she asked, directing her question to Maggie.

"All but Sam and Rosie," her husband said.

Maggie nodded. "It seats twenty. Quite something. I'll bet if you asked, he'd send it back for you whenever want to visit the Valley."

Her husband grinned. "In a heartbeat. So Tim, what's your occupation?

"Woodworker and lobsterman, depending on the season."

"His work is extraordinary," Rich said. "You should take a look while you're here. Dad has one of his pieces in the house."

"I'd love to see them," Maggie said.

"Tim also helps the Lab to track poachers of our most famous native species, the horseshoe crab," Gail said. "We actually saw some poachers on our boat ride this morning."

There ensued a long discussion of the issues surrounding the poaching and dwindling population of the crabs. At one point, Maggie said, "The kids would love to see a horseshoe crab. Are they easy to find along the shore?"

"Sometimes," Tim said. "I'd be happy to take them out on the river if you have time this weekend. I know a bunch of their secret hideouts."

"It's a plan, buddy. Just tell us the time and place, and we'll be there," Ben Morgan said.

Tim and he made a plan to meet Friday morning as the staff passed desserts. Gail's brothers also expressed interest in joining them. Maggie and Rose had plans to go into town with Gail and her sisters.

As the evening wore down, Tim and Gail strolled the edge of the group hand in hand. "I'd better hightail it," he said. "Early day tomorrow. I'll go out at first light, then come back and get the Morgan crew at ten."

"You're a good soul, Tim Miller."

"I love taking people out."

She walked him to the truck, and he pulled her into the shadows for a lingering, toe-curling kiss. "I'd like nothing better than to take this further," he said, "but with all these Morgans prowling around…"

"Agree!" She smiled up at him in the darkness. "Night."

As she headed back to join the others, she found Pam, Weezie, Maggie, and Rose talking on the porch. Ruthie Morgan, the younger cousin, ran by chasing her toddler, Charlotte, her brother Kyle in hot pursuit. "Some things never change," Maggie said, shaking her head.

Beth Morgan joined them. "Our sister still hasn't grown up." Her toddler, Lily, wriggled out of her arms and ran toward the others. Ben and Maggie's son, Bennie, was in the midst of the melee, as were the family patriarch, Ben Senior, and Ben and Maggie's daughter Emma.

"And we love her for it," Rose said.

"Oh, yes we do!" Weezie said. "Now where's Hope? We need to plan our ladies' outing tomorrow. Since we were forbidden to have any bachelor or bachelorette parties, we have to do something really cool with you all. Show you around. We can probably drag Harriet and Lynn in too. Lucy's arranged a bunch of babysitters at her house for all the kiddies."

They decided upon a drive up the coast and around the peninsula, then lunch at the Cove Grille and maybe a stroll along Main Street.

As Maggie and Ben said good night, she caught Gail at the door. "Your guy seems great. Have you been together long?"

Gail smiled. "Less than a week."

Maggie's eyes widened in surprise. "Wow, it looked like… Well, you have chemistry, that's for sure."

"It's been kind of a whirlwind," Gail said, surprised she was confiding to someone she'd just met. She found herself drawn to the other's warmth.

Maggie hugged her. "Hope it continues. You both seem very happy together."

"Thanks. See you tomorrow."

Gail headed inside to join her siblings in the family room. *Hope it continues. Me too!*

CHAPTER 16

Friday flew by in happy chaos as Gail and her sisters shepherded the Morgan women around. She had never had many women friends, but found she enjoyed the company of the diverse, friendly group of women. Beth and Rose were quiet, Maggie warm and gregarious. Hope, Robbie Morgan's wife and a well-known painter, was ethereal, with long blonde hair and pale blue eyes, and Ruthie Morgan and her sister, Weezie, were clones. Harriet and Lynn joined them for lunch along with Harriet's sisters Clara and Hazel.

That evening, the family and a few friends celebrated at Ballard's. The restaurant's large function room was beautifully decorated with flowers and greenery. As Gail stood watching the crowd, her father approached and put his arm around her shoulder. "You could've asked him tonight too, baby. There's plenty of room."

She rested her head against his chest. "Thanks, Dad, but he'll be here tomorrow. That's probably enough of our big crazy bunch for him."

"You like him, don't you?"

She nodded but said nothing.

He patted her back. "Good man. Solid and steady. I like him too."

"Let's not get too attached yet. Okay?"

"What'd you think of all your cousins?"

Gail smiled as little Bennie ran by and disappeared under a table. "I love them all. I can't believe they've been out there all this time and we never knew them."

"My fault, baby. Never kept up with my brother and Leonora. Big mistake. Love 'em to pieces."

"They're great, and Spark too."

"Now, he's a keeper. Has great kids too, Buck the artist and Amy. They're part of the family too."

"Do they both live in the Valley?"

Richard shook his head, waving to Lucy, who stood across the room. "Doesn't she look stunning?"

"Sure does."

"Now, what did you ask? Oh yeah, Buck Foster's in Los Angeles, and Amy lives in Saguaro Valley. When she came out with her dad, she fell in love with the young, handsome cowpoke Jeb Barnes, who works for Maggie at Morgan's Run."

"Cowpoke? Really, Dad, you've been watching too many old Westerns."

"And you, my darling girl, have not been to Saguaro Valley. Place is thick with cowpokes. No other name for 'em. Maggie's dad, Ned Williams, is one of the most famous wranglers the Southwest has ever produced. He's a cowpoke through and through."

"And an excellent veterinarian, according to Kyle."

"Yup. Will you excuse me, darling? I'd like to check in with my bride."

"Sure," she said, as Richard hurried across the room to Lucy. Her soon-to-be stepmother looked glorious in a silver sheath that hugged her slender frame.

"There goes a happy man," her brother Wolfie said, coming to stand beside her.

Gail nodded. "That he is."

"You've gotten over the whole 'I hate Lucy' thing, haven't you?"

Gail cringed, recalling her infantile behavior when her father and Lucy first started dating. "I was an asshole. I've apologized. We're friends."

"Good," he said, arm around her shoulder. Wolfie was a man of few words, but when he spoke, he meant every word. Currently, he worked for Lucy and her partner in their book business and also rented the apartment above her garage.

Their father was hoping he'd step in and run the Morgan's Fire vineyard, but so far, Wolfie had not given him an answer yes or no.

"You know Lang, Beth's husband, and his sister Rose's parents run a vineyard?" He nodded. "Wish I'd visited when we were out there."

"You could go back. Maybe there's room on Spark's plane?"

"We'll see. I'm still trying to decide if I want to get sucked back into the maw."

Gail elbowed him. "Not fair. Besides, *I'm* part of that maw, you know!"

"Excluding you," he said as their father called for everyone to find their places for dinner.

Gail followed him to his seat. *Maw indeed!*

*****

After a long day, Tim and Coop went to the grille for dinner. They sat at the bar and chatted with bartender Vincent Rodriguez, son of the owners. They'd gone to school with the dark-haired young man who had published three successful short story collections, two of which had won major awards. As Vinnie moved off to put in their dinner orders and wait on others, Coop said, "Okay, buddy, spit it out. You've been clammed up for two days. I feel like I'm working alongside a two-by-four."

"Ha-ha."

Coop eyed his friend. "How'd the boat ride go?"

"Great, the kids loved it."

"I'm not talking about today," Coop said, catching Vinnie's eye and pointing to his empty beer mug.

"That was fine too, until we ran into that boatload of scum."

"I'm not asking about the pirates of the peninsula. I'm wondering how things went with Gail? Your girlfriend?"

"She's great."

"And?"

"And that's all. We've been on three dates. Four if you count the family dinner and last night's barbecue."

"She's hot," Coop said. "Oops, did I say that out loud?"

"Yes, and you're right. Now can we please talk about something else?"

*****

When he got home that night, the lock to his apartment was scratched and the doorjamb too. Cautiously, he tried the door. Still locked. Even though nothing in the apartment had been disturbed, a sinking feeling lodged in his gut, and he slept fitfully. When he got to the barn, Coop was standing in his workshop with two local cops at his side.

"We've been robbed, buddy. Cash box gone and a bunch of tools."

"Unusual for the village," Officer Pete Avery said, shaking his head. His associate Bobby Moniz stood beside him, scanning the room. Pete and Bobby had gone to school with Tim's sister Karen. They were the only people besides Coop who knew about Izzy's drug habit.

Pete looked up at Tim. "I hate to say it, buddy, but you know who this looks like."

"She wouldn't do something like this," he said, turning away and slamming out of the shop.

Coop reached out and grasped Bobby's arm when he started to go after Tim. "Let him go, man. He'll come around. It was only a few hundred dollars. The tools are insured."

Tim jumped into the truck and started cruising aimlessly up and down Main Street, then out the Point Road. *Where is she? If it was Izzy, she couldn't have done it alone.*

CHAPTER 17

Tim spent the next day continuing to search the village, checking all the familiar places where she might go, with no luck. Finally, at three, he returned to the apartment and dressed for the wedding. It was the last thing he wanted to do, but he didn't want to stand Gail up. He'd go, have a few dances, avoid Coop as much as possible, then head back and search some more.

He and Gail had arranged to find each other at the meeting house at Hampton Meeting School, where the wedding ceremony was to take place. Tim parked at the edge of campus and walked the short distance across the green to the simple chapel, its white clapboards freshly painted, two wreaths of blue hydrangeas on either side of the doors. The day was warm, and he already felt stifled in his dark gray suit. He rarely dressed up and found the whole process unpleasant. However, when he spied her on the meeting house steps, all thoughts of his discomfort vanished.

Gail shimmered in a pale pink off-the-shoulder gown. Thin ribbons of draped sleeves framed the low neckline. The airy chiffon gown was shaped with densely ruched panels wrapped round the bodice. From the neck to her ass, the dress hugged every inch of her, the skirt flaring out below. The effect was ravishing. "You look beyond beautiful."

"I hope that's a good thing?" she replied.

He wore dark suit, white shirt and blue tie. "Most definitely a good thing." Tim hugged her, whispering, "Only thing that would make this moment perfect would be if I could whip off that amazing dress and make love to you."

Gail smiled, so pleased at his reaction. As they started in, she gazed over and was surprised to see what appeared to be anger in his dark eyes. "What is it? Is everything okay?"

When he looked down, the warmth had returned. "Fine, no worries."

There was something troubling him, and this was only confirmed an hour later when they walked into the reception and ran into Coop. Tim's friend was not entirely successful in hiding his concern. "Hey, buddy, doin' okay?"

Tim nodded. "Fine. Hey, what can I get you to drink?" he asked, turning to her.

She asked for white wine, and Tim headed off, his friend on his heels. *Whatever's wrong, Coop knows about it.*

"Hey, sis, photos!" Weezie grabbed her arm. "They're going to try to get all the Morgans together."

*****

"Aren't they a handsome couple," Leonora Morgan said as she and Gail stood watching Richard twirling Lucy around for their first dance.

Gail nodded. "Sure are. Just like you and Uncle Ben. What's your secret?"

"Oh, honey, tough to analyze what makes for a happy marriage. From the moment I saw Ben, I knew he was the one, and he felt the same way. We tell each other how much we love each other all the time, at least ten times a day. Ben's my dearest friend, my boyfriend, and the love of my life. Our bond gets stronger every year watching our kids and grandkids. We're truly blessed, just like your family. And you seem to have found a great guy. I enjoyed talking to your Tim. Ben had a ball on the ride up the river, and he and I visited his workshop this morning with Richard."

"Oh?"

"What exquisite work he does. Even in the chaos of the break-in, he showed us around. That nice blacksmith too. I ordered seven lamps from him, one for us and each of our kids."

Gail stared at her aunt. "Break-in?"

"Didn't he mention it? Probably didn't want to spoil the wedding. Someone broke in and stole some tools and money, I believe. I didn't want to pry, but the police were there, so Tim mentioned it."

"Hey, honey, how about a spin around the floor?" Ben Senior asked, hugging his wife.

Leonora stood on tiptoes and kissed his cheek. "Oh pish tush. We spin around every day. What about your beautiful niece here?"

The handsome silver-haired patriarch extended his hand. "I'd be delighted."

Gail smiled. "I wouldn't hear of it. You two dance. I've got to find someone anyway."

"Hope it's that handsome fella of yours," he said. "He's a keeper. Come on, Nora, they're playin' our song."

As the elder Morgans strolled off arm in arm, Gail scanned the room. Finally, she spotted Coop by the bar talking to her brother Teddy. She couldn't see Tim anywhere. *I've got to know,* she thought, heading toward the bar. When she reached the two men, Teddy said, "Hey, sis, where's the fire?"

"Nowhere, but I'd love it if you could get me a white wine?"

Teddy gave her a puzzled look, then shrugged. "Sure thing."

When he was out of earshot, she turned to Coop. "Where's Tim? I can't seem to find him."

Coop looked ready to bolt. "I think he stepped out to make a phone call, maybe? Should be back in a sec."

"Coop, what's wrong?"

He reddened, clearing his throat and gazing around the room. "Not sure what you mean."

"Yes, you do. Please tell me."

"I can't. It's…well, there's nothing to tell. Just guesses."

"I heard about the break-in."

"Not a big deal. We'll survive."

Gail stared hard at him, wondering if she was crossing a line. Then she took a breath and said, "Does he think it's her?"

Coop nodded. "But that's not unusual. He sees Izzy in every shadow, every day. It was probably just kids."

"But clearly you don't think so, and neither does he."

"It's kind of her MO, if you know what I mean. Grab and dash."

"But no sign of her?"

"Nope, and here comes the man now. Gonna grab a beer for me and him."

Teddy handed her the wine. "Thanks," she said, setting it on a nearby table as she went to meet Tim.

"Everything okay?"

He paused, studying her, then said, "Yeah, great. Want to dance?"

CHAPTER 18

Tim held out his hand and she took it, allowing him to lead her to the dance floor just as a new slow song began, Rod Stewart's "Have I Told You Lately." As he drew her close, Gail breathed a sigh of relief, resting her head on his chest.

"You sure you're okay?" she asked.

"Am now," he said.

Tears sprang to Gail's eyes. She'd fallen hard for Tim Miller, and now it could all be taken away. Coop's words echoed as they moved together in perfect harmony. *He sees Izzy in every shadow.*

The song ended, and he said, "Want a drink?"

"Not especially. You?"

Arm around her shoulders, he looked down at her. "Walk?"

"Perfect."

After leaving the reception in the Persimmon Room, they strolled down the halls of Netherfield Manor and out the front door. "This is quite a place, isn't it?"

She nodded.

"We had a family reunion here last year. Mavis gave my parents the Darn Yarner discount. Was cool."

"Mavis must lose a lot of money if she gives discounts to all the yarners," Gail said.

"I'm sure she more than makes up for it with all her celebrity clients. There've been a ton of them over the years. It's been a huge boon to the village economy."

As it was a warm spring evening, they walked down a path that led to one of the cottages. Along the way, a trellis led into a rose garden lined with teak benches. "Oh, this is lovely," she said, gazing around.

"Not as lovely as you," he said, smiling. "Here, let's sit a minute." He led her to a bench, and they sat side by side, his arm still around her. Gail leaned against him, drinking in his warmth and strength, wondering if it might soon be withdrawn forever.

"I guess you might have heard about the break-in at the shop. Your family was in this morning."

She sat up and looked at him, drawing away from his embrace. "Was it last night, then?"

"Night before. Police were back today to look things over and talk to me."

"Oh?"

"There were some indicators. I mean, we might have dismissed it as kids, but someone tried, unsuccessfully, to break into my apartment that same night."

Gail studied him. He looked ten years older, the weight of the world on his broad, strong shoulders. "So you think it might be her?"

He shrugged. "Could be. Not alone, but yes, it could be."

She took his hand. "Is there anything I can do?"

When he looked up, his eyes were rimmed with tears. "No, thanks. I just wanted you to know. Izzy's my problem. I'll deal with it. I didn't want you to hear about this from someone else. I care about you, Gail, a lot, but this might get rough. I'd understand if you wanted to say 'see ya later, buddy,' and part of me wants to suggest you do just that. The other part of me thinks I'd go crazy without you."

"Well, I'm not going anywhere."

"Thanks, but I'll understand if you change your mind."

She didn't know what to say, so she put her arms around him. "I'm here, and I'm going to stay here."

Stiffly, he returned her embrace, then stood. "Come on. Let's get you back to the party."

"Are you sure?"

"Absolutely. If you're up for it, I'd love one more slow dance, then Coop and I are going to take off."

"Do you want me to come with you?"

"No way. This is your dad's wedding. You belong here with your family. Come on." He took her hand, and they walked back in silence. They entered the Persimmon Room to the strains of Marvin Gaye's "Let's Get It On." "Wouldn't I love that," he said, sweeping her into his arms.

Gail closed her eyes and gave herself over to the music and Tim's warmth and strength. *Let this not be the end of us. Please, please, not the end!*

After Tim's departure, the evening wore down. Most villagers had departed, but the family remained. Richard and Lucy were leaving for the Seychelles Monday so they could spend the next day with the cousins. Toddlers had been put to sleep in other rooms of the house, and parents danced or sat around chatting.

Pam found Gail in the kitchen, chatting with Kendall Reese, the chef. "Hey, ladies, is this hangout central?"

Gail gave her a weary smile. "No, just wanted to compliment Kendall on the incredible food."

"It was delicious," Pam said. "Everything."

Kendall nodded. "Thanks. We aim to please."

The sisters said good night and walked back to the reception together. "I don't know about you," Pam said, "but I'm not sure I can keep up with the West Coast Morgans."

Gail smiled. "They are quite a lively bunch, even the elders."

"Aunt Leonora just made Uncle Ben leave."

"I know. Dad says he has a heart condition," Gail said.

"Well, you'd never know it to see him on the dance floor. Are you doing okay, sis?"

Gail rested her head on Pam's shoulder. "Truthfully, I've been better."

"What happened to Tim?"

"It's a long story, and I'm not sure I'm at liberty to say anything. Suffice to say that tonight might well have been our last dance." Tears spilled down her cheeks, and she brushed them away.

Pam hugged her. "Oh no, that can't be. Come here."

After returning her sister's hug, Gail broke away. "Let's not make a scene. This is Dad and Lucy's night. I'm a big girl, and I'm going to pull myself together, enjoy our crazy cousins, and fall apart after they leave."

Pam smiled. "Come on, then. I think Kyle and our crazy youngest brother are cooking something up over there."

"Thanks, sis," Gail said, meeting the other's eyes before being pulled back into the fray.

CHAPTER 19

The hall light was out again, so Tim climbed the stairs to his apartment in darkness, lights from the occasional passing car shining through the stairwell windows. When he reached the second floor, he sensed immediately that he was not alone. Her presence was palpable, even though he couldn't see her in the darkness. He pulled out his cell phone and shone the flashlight down the narrow hallway. She leaned against his door, crumpled in an impossibly small heap.

"Iz?" he said softly.

She stirred. Back against the door, arms outstretched, she slowly inched her way up like a spider until she stood facing him.

He stepped around her and unlocked the door, swinging it open and feeling for the light switch. "Come in," he said as light revealed her pale, sepulchral face and rail-thin body. Shocked, he touched her shoulder. "What's going on? Come on, sit. Want something to eat?"

"I need money," she mumbled, voice raspy, gruff.

He watched her slump onto the sofa. Her skin hung on her bones. Her clothes were worn and dirty. "You need to eat," he said, moving to the refrigerator. "What do you want? I've got cheese, bread, eggs, cereal. I could make you an omelet."

She raised a weak, birdlike arm. "Stop it Tim. Just stop it. I don't want to eat. I need money."

"For?"

"For none of your goddamn business."

"Well, I'm not giving you money. I'll feed you and get you help, but I'm not supporting your drug habit. Jesus Christ, Izzy. I haven't seen you in ten years, and you show up asking for drug money? Who's with you?"

"No one."

"Bullshit. I know you and someone broke into the barn. How'd you even know about that, anyway?"

"Aunt Mae gives…gave me occasional updates. Your furniture is beautiful, by way. Always knew you were talented."

Tim studied her, wondering if he'd have even recognized her had they passed on the street. Probably not unless he heard her voice. Even her eyes had changed. Her lovely blue eyes, once clear, were now cloudy. *Dead eyes.* Her voice was coarser, rougher, but still had the familiar timbre, that sexy huskiness that had once lit him up like a firecracker. "Where have you been for the past decade?" he asked.

"Can we talk about this in the morning? I slept on the ground last night, and I'm beyond tired. Okay if I crash on your sofa?"

He nodded, noticing a small tattered backpack on the floor beside her. "You need anything? Want a shower?"

"In the morning," she said already lying back, closing her eyes. "You look like a million bucks, by the way. How was the big wedding?"

He wanted to ask how she knew about the wedding, but instead went to his bedroom and grabbed a quilt from the closet. When he returned, she was snoring. He covered her gently and turned out the light. After which he sat in an armchair opposite, watching her. *Ten years. The woman he had loved, a stranger. A stranger, thief, and drug addict.*

*****

Tim's apartment faced east, so the morning light streamed into his living room, hitting the chair where he'd slept. He started awake and found the sofa empty, quilt tossed to the floor. Thinking she'd vanished, he felt his heart constrict, but the sound of the shower curtain being pulled back let him know she was still there. He looked around, hoping to search through her backpack for answers, but she had taken it into the bathroom. Still in his suit, tie loose around his neck, he shook his head. *What the hell am I doing? I should call the cops and turn her in.*

A few minutes later, she appeared, dressed in his bathrobe, a towel on her head. "This okay?" she asked, pointing to the robe. Scrubbed and clean, she looked more like herself, albeit a skeletal version.

"Sure, of course. You're not gonna run out on me if I hop in the shower, are you?"

"Not if you have coffee."

He led her into the kitchen and showed her where things were. As he turned away, he saw her hands shaking violently as she scooped coffee into the machine. When he returned dressed in jeans and a T-shirt, Izzy sat at the small kitchen table, drinking coffee and reading yesterday's newspaper. Her faded T-shirt and torn jeans hung on her impossibly thin frame, hair limp and lifeless. Izzy's yellow skin was blotched with sores and what looked like old scars. Tim stared at the young woman he'd loved for most of his youth and wondered if anything remained of her underneath the withered shell.

"Hey," he said softly.

A tremor ran through her as she looked up at him with bloodshot eyes. She was in major withdrawal, and it would only get worse. "I'm gonna take off pretty soon."

"Don't," he said, sitting down beside her. "Stay here, and we'll get you help."

"I can't."

Her hand was like ice when he grabbed hold of it. "Please Iz, let me help you."

"No, baby. As you said last night, it's been ten years. I've moved on, and so have you."

"That doesn't mean I don't care about you."

"Don't say that. I'm with someone now."

"Who, another junkie?"

"Does it matter?" she said softly.

"To me it does. Why don't you let me help you? I have some money saved. We can get you checked into rehab, get you clean, then see from there."

"Stop, Tim!" She gulped her coffee and stood up. "I've gotta go."

"Where are the tools. Sold?"

She shrugged. "He handles that."

"I want them back. Tell your boyfriend I'll buy them back for more than he can get pawning them."

"Maybe. I don't suppose you could spare a little of that cash now?"

"Eat this bagel if you want money," he said, pulling a cinnamon raisin bagel from a bag he'd bought the previous afternoon.

She took a small bite. "A little stale."

"Eat or no cash."

Slowly, she nibbled her way through the bread. When she finished, she threw out her hands. "Ta-da!"

He emptied his wallet, giving her sixty dollars. "Have a meal with that, not smack."

She pocketed the money and slung the backpack over her shoulder. "I'll be in touch."

"You got a phone?"

"A burner."

"What's the number?"

She handed him the phone. He programmed his number in, then noted hers. "You promise you'll call."

"No promises."

"Izzy, please."

"I'll talk to Ice and see what he says."

"Ice? What kind of a name is that? What's his real name?"

She patted his cheek. "Less you know, the better, baby."

And then she was gone. Like a wisp of smoke, she vanished leaving him cold and confused. He contemplated following her, but instead grabbed his jacket and headed for the docks.

CHAPTER 20

Sunday was a blur of Morgans with a brunch at the farmhouse catered by Callie with pastries and canisters of hot beverages from the café in town. Gail enjoyed the time with her cousins, but in the back of her mind was Tim and the mysterious woman from his past. She checked her phone continuously, but he neither called nor texted. Finally, she called, and his phone went straight to voicemail. She left a short message telling him she was thinking about him.

Sunday evening, the family gathered for one last meal, a clambake at the Salters' farm in Bayshore just south of Horseshoe Crab Cove. "They have it down to a science," Lucy had told them as they planned the weekend. "So much easier to have it at their place."

She was right. They sat at long tables under a huge tent, enjoying chowder and fritters, then a full bake. When popsicles were served at the end of the meal, several people rose to give toasts.

Ben Morgan Senior led them off. "Well, little brother," he said, grinning at the newlyweds. "You've certainly outdone yourself. And I thought we did things big in the Valley. We're really gonna have to up our game, aren't we, Nora? Spark?"

"Here, here!" his friend called. "Nothin' better than a good challenge."

The family patriarch gazed down at his wife. "On behalf of our family, Nora and I want to thank Richard, Lucy, and all the folks back here for the time of a lifetime. Haven't spent much time back East, but after bein' here in this slice of paradise, I guarantee we'll be back. And we're lookin' forward to hostin' you all out in Saguaro in December for Harriet and Kyle's weddin'. Think of it as a wedding week and plan to stay as long as you can. I want to also thank everyone for welcoming our youngest son into this amazin' community. If we can't have him back with us—and we miss him a lot—we're mighty glad he found such a loving home here with all of you good people."

A number of others spoke, then Gail unexpectedly found herself standing as if driven by an unseen force. She clicked her glass and cleared her throat. "I know, I know, big surprise, me standing up. I'll be brief. My toast is actually for Lucy. As some of you may know, when Dad first started seeing Lucy, I was kind of an asshole. No, that's wrong. I wasn't kind of an asshole. I was a big asshole.

"I did everything I could to warn Lucy off, scare her away, break them up. I can see from your faces how truly shocking my behavior was. I want to say again, as I've said to whoever will listen—I was wrong, wrong, wrong. Lucy and Dad are perfect together. I was too young to really remember much about my mom and about my parents' relationship, but I have watched my dad over the last two decades, and I've never seen him happy like he is now. Lucy, what a remarkable gift you are to this family. You have truly changed Dad's life and ours, and I love you very much." Tears streamed down her face as she sat down.

Richard hopped up and came to throw his arms around her. "Oh, princess, we love you so."

Lucy was right behind him. After they hugged, she whispered, "You okay? If you need to talk, I'm here."

Gail smiled. "I'm fine. You're on your honeymoon, remember?"

Her father overheard the word honeymoon and turned to the group. "Speaking of the honeymoon, my beautiful bride and I leave for the Seychelles in the morning, so we may not see everyone again. I wish you safe travels on Foster Airlines, and we hope you come back very soon."

*****

"So that was quite a weekend," Ava said as the four sisters sat together in the farmhouse great room Monday evening. Dan was home with the kids, and their brothers had departed.

Pam nodded. "Sure was. Can't believe Dad waited all these years for us to meet our cousins. I'm excited about going out there next winter."

"It's very cool," Weezie said. "And so many gorgeous cowboys."

Ava gazed over at Gail. "Speaking of gorgeous. What's up with Tim? He left the wedding pretty early, didn't he?"

"He's embroiled in something right now," Gail said.

Weezie stared at her. "What kind of something?"

"I can't say too much because I promised I wouldn't, but an old girlfriend may be back in the area."

"What do you mean may?" Ava asked. "Is she or isn't she?"

Gail shook her head. "I don't know. He didn't know the last time I spoke to him, and that was Saturday night."

Pam studied her sister, who appeared on the verge of tears, then hopped up. "Who's in the mood for leftovers?"

Her sisters followed her into the kitchen, and they began rummaging in cupboards and the fridge. Casseroles, appetizers, and an array of salads were spread on the island, and the four sat on stools, forks in hand. "Think Dad and Lucy are there yet?" Ava asked, eyes dreamy. "I'd love to be in the Seychelles."

"They don't get in until tomorrow," Gail said. "Long trip for only a week there."

"I loved your speech, sis," Pam said, patting Gail's arm.

"So did Dad," Weezie said. "You kind of brought down the house. Everyone was crying by the end."

Gail shrugged. "Had to be said."

"And you said it well," Ava replied. "I'm sure Tim'll figure things out too. He's a great guy. Steady as a rock and so talented."

"Maybe," Gail said, "but as we know, I don't have much luck in affairs of the heart."

"You really like him, then?" Weezie asked.

Gail nodded, a lump in her throat.

"Hey, ladies. Let's throw all this back in the fridge and take a walk," Pam suggested.

Gail said a silent thank-you as they grabbed sweaters and jackets and headed out arm in arm. *That's right. One foot in front of the other. You can do it. Every day will get easier.*

CHAPTER 21

Tuesday morning, Gail was alone in the house, Weezie at the stables, Pam looking at rental properties, and Callie in town shopping. She worked in the office for a few hours, her cell phone beside her. Silent. Finally unable to take another moment of wondering, she pushed back her office chair and stood. *That's it, I've got to see him one way or the other!*

She drove into town and parked alongside the barn. Tim's truck was gone, but Coop's was there. She found him in the workshop, hammering a curved leg for a floor lamp. "Hey, Coop," she called, trying not to startle him.

He glanced up but kept at it for several minutes until he was satisfied. He then set hammer and lamp base aside. "He's not here."

"I can see that."

"Gail, I think I know why you're here, but I don't know what to tell you. I've barely seen him. He's on the river now, but he hasn't been here for days."

"What about her?"

Coop shrugged.

"Please, I'm going crazy."

"She's around. I know that much, but that's it."

"Is she out on the boat with him?"

"Doubt it."

"Okay, sorry to bother you. I'll let you get back to work, but if you see him, please tell him I stopped by."

"Will do. Gail, he cares about you. I know he does. I think he just has to work this out, then he'll be in touch."

"What does work things out even mean?"

He shrugged. "Hard to say. It's pretty fucked up. She messes with his head. Always has. Just gotta hope that she's out of his system."

"But she isn't, is she?"

Gail headed for the door, trying hard not to burst into tears. Before she reached it, the door swung open and two people appeared. One, an impossibly thin blonde in tattered skinny jeans and a Wesleyan sweatshirt Gail recognized. *Tim's.* Her companion was wiry and dark, with tattoos covering his arms, face, and neck. He held a circular saw in one hand and what looked like a planer in the other. She carried a wooden box with a leather handle.

"Izzy, long time no see," Coop said.

"This him?" her companion said.

Izzy shook her head. "Where's Tim?"

"Out," Coop said. "Nice of you to bring those back. Have you got the rest?"

"Tim promised he'd leave money for these," she said, her hands shaking.

"Well, since you guys took all our petty cash, there's no money here," Coop said. "Why don't you set those down, go get the rest, and beat it. If it's all here, we won't call the cops."

"Fuck you, man. That wasn't the deal."

"Ice, stop it. Not helpful," she said.

"Izzy, what the hell?" Coop said. "How did you get mixed up with this slimeball?"

"Shut the fuck up," Ice said. "Either you and Ms. Prom Queen over here pay up, or we're outta here."

Coop turned as if remembering Gail's presence for the first time. "As I said, we don't have any cash, and the lady was just leaving." He motioned with his head for her to move.

"Like hell she is." Ice pulled a knife from his pocket.

Her whole body trembling, Izzy dropped the wooden box, which broke open, spilling tools to the barn floor. "Stop it!" she cried, lunging at Ice, but Coop beat her to it. Hammer in one hand and what looked like a wrought iron spear in the other, he slammed down on the arm that held the knife, and it clattered to the floor and slid under a workbench.

Gail jumped back as the two men wrestled. Ice was quick, but Coop was quicker and much stronger. Within minutes, he had him pinned on the floor, his knee on his back.

Coop turned to her. "Call 911, then fish under there for the knife."

As Gail fumbled in her bag, Izzy ran out the door.

By the time the police arrived, Izzy had vanished. Gail and Coop followed the two officers as they led Ice out in handcuffs. A battered van was parked in the lot.

"That theirs?" Pete Aviary asked.

Coop stared at it. "Piece of crap sure isn't mine. This isn't either." He handed Ice's knife to Bobby.

"The van wasn't there when I arrived," Gail said.

Bobby Moniz headed for the van as Pete shoved Ice into the cruiser. Bobby threw open the back. Along with a dirty mattress and blankets, they spied more tools, trash bags, and several televisions.

Bobby whistled. "Looks like someone's been camping out with a shitload of stolen crap."

"Where's Izzy?" Pete asked.

Coop gave him a look. "Took off. She's nothing. You've got the lowlife sleazebag that did this."

Pete gazed around, perhaps expecting Izzy to jump out of the bushes. "You know we can't leave it at that, Coop. If you see her, you call. Got it? We'll send someone back for the van as soon as we dump him."

The cruiser disappeared, leaving Gail and Coop standing side by side. "Sorry you had to be here for that."

Shaken and numb, Gail looked at him, eyes wide. "What will happen to them?"

"Who knows, who cares."

"But he does care, doesn't he? About her at least."

"It's complicated. You okay?"

She nodded. "Do you think I should stay?"

"No, if they want ask you any questions, they know where to find you. Go on home."

"And Coop—"

"I'll tell him you stopped by. I'm sure he'll be in touch."

CHAPTER 22

Shattered, Gail headed to her car. She didn't know where to go or what to do. She couldn't go home to an empty house. Passing by her car, she walked the short distance to Main Street, then down to the side door of Cove Toys and Games. She climbed the stairs to the second-floor office of Merlin's Closet, relieved to find her brother working alone.

Gail had only been to Lucy's office once. This was the headquarters of Merlin's Closet, the children's book company owned by her stepmother and Lolly LaSalle. It was a small but profitable operation with a storage barn on Mavis LaSalle's estate for use when they received large shipments for the book fairs they ran in local communities. Wolfie Morgan worked part-time for them.

He gazed up from the floor amidst a pile of picture books. "Hey, sis, what brings you up here?"

Gail plopped down beside him and leaned back against a stack of boxes. "I've just had the weirdest experience, and I didn't know where to go."

Wolfie studied her face, then set his work aside. "You okay? You're white as a ghost."

"That's because I've just seen a ghost, sort of."

She knew she shouldn't say anything about Izzy, but she trusted her siblings implicitly. If she told Wolfie, it would go no further. He listened quietly as she related the incident at the workshop and the story of Tim's unfortunate girlfriend. When she concluded, she said, "So here I am, leaning on my baby brother 'cause I can't face going home."

He scooted nearer and opened his arms. As Gail fell into his strong embrace, the floodgates opened. All the pent-up emotions of the morning and the past several days spilled over.

"Hey, hey, sis. It's gonna be okay."

After a few minutes, she patted his shoulders and sat back, wiping her eyes. "This is what I get for dating!"

"Bullshit. Dating's good. Tim's a great guy. This isn't his fault or yours. He'll get it straightened out. Sounds like this Izzy is pretty fucked up. Safest place for her is probably jail, if they catch her."

"Not for a former cop."

"Sounds like that's ancient history."

"I don't think hardened criminals keep track of history. All they care about is what she was."

"When did you get to be an expert on hardened criminals?"

She smiled. "I watch a lot of police shows."

"Well, maybe there's a way to protect her from the hardened criminals."

"Wolfie, her friend had a knife and God knows what else! What if they'd had a gun or he'd stabbed Coop or me?"

"But he didn't," he said, taking her hands. "Hey, you know what? I forgot to pack lunch today. Why don't we grab something at the Café? We can compare notes on the vineyard. I promised Dad I'd make a decision about jumping in after the honeymoon."

Gail looked over his shoulder and spied his canvas lunch bag. "You're a terrible liar, brother dear. Why don't you bring your macrobiotic crap, and you can watch me eat my BLT."

He grinned, the same killer smile as all the Morgan men. "I was thinking I'd get the super Reuben, actually."

As they strolled Main Street arm in arm, she said, "You know you're going to have to say yes to Dad, don't you? You can't leave me there with Weezie and Rich. I need you."

"When has anyone ever been able to say no to Dad?"

Gail smiled, looking over at him. "You have, for one. Lucy, for a while, at least."

"*Really* said no, I mean."

"No one. You're right. Even Lucy caved, as you will too. You'll be great out there, by the way. The tasting rooms and gallery are going to be so cool. Dad's already got us booked for a stop on next year's Coastal Wines Tour. Never mind that we may not be operational by then."

"That's Dad," he said, opening the Café door.

"Yes, it is. Thanks, dearie," she said, patting his arm as they headed into the crowded, light-filled restaurant.

"Anytime. Can't wait for my Reuben."

*****

"Jesus Christ, Coop. Why didn't you call?" Tim paced the shop, running fingers through his thick, rumpled hair.

His friend set down his hammer. "Well, for one thing, we were kinda busy with your ex and her whack-job, coked-up friend. For another, there wasn't much you could do from out on the river."

"Where'd she go?"

"Which one?"

"You know damn well I mean Gail."

"Dunno. Her car was in the lot until an hour ago. Maybe she went shopping, then headed home. Have you called her?"

Tim plunked down on a half-finished bench. "What the hell would I say? Sorry my girlfriend almost got you killed?"

"Ex-girlfriend."

"Whatever. You know what I mean. Don't suppose you know where *she* went either?"

"Not a clue, and no offense, buddy, I'd like to keep it that way. She's one fucked-up broad. Looks about eighty. Was shakin' like a leaf."

"Now, without him, she's not likely to score anytime soon. Geez, what a nightmare."

Coop came and sat beside him, gazing straight ahead. "Look, buddy, I said it ten years ago, and I'll say it again now. You gotta let her go. Izzy's a lost soul who doesn't give a shit about you or anyone. I know, I know… She wasn't like that. But heroin took the Izzy you knew away, and she ain't comin' back."

Elbows on knees, Tim put his head down. "If she could only get clean."

"Would you want her back?"

"At least I'd know she was okay."

"Gail's a great person. If she's the one, terrific. If she isn't, I guarantee that Izzy Hodge isn't either. Cut her loose."

"I have."

"Uh huh, was that at the same time you told her you'd pay them to bring back our stuff?"

"Okay, okay. I need a shower."

"You comin' back here today?"

"Not sure. I'm going down to the police station, then we'll see."

"No need. They have the sleazeball and their ratty van."

Tim stood, eyeing his friend. "You know I already have a mother and father."

"Who would tell you the same thing. Stay away from anything that has to do with her."

"See you, Coop. And if by some chance you run into anyone in my family, not a word about this."

"This is Horseshoe Crab Cove, buddy. Everyone'll know about this by tonight except Richard and Lucy Morgan, who are eight thousand miles away. Come to think of it, the gossip hotline might just reach them over there too."

Tim slammed the barn door. *Great, just great! After ten years, I've met an amazing woman. Now she probably hates my guts, the whole town knows about Izzy, and I'm about to go stark raving mad!*

CHAPTER 23

When Tim pulled his truck up beside his building, he spied his father in the shadows, sitting on a broken lawn chair. Rex Miller stood. Six four, with thick dark hair more pepper than salt and the sinewy strong built of the farmer he was, he looked a decade younger than his sixty-five years. "Hey, son."

Tim hugged him. "Hey, Dad."

"Your mom sent me."

"Of course she did."

"She's worried. We're worried."

"Well, don't be. I'm handling it."

"Got a beer for your old man?"

"Come on," Tim said. "Mind if I jump in the shower first? My skin's crawling from the salt water."

Rex followed him up the stairs to the apartment. "You been out today, then?"

"Yup."

"Any sign of the poachers?"

"No, but I got a good catch and also dumped a bunch of their traps."

"Good on ya."

"Been watching Mom's Australian soap operas again?"

Rex laughed. "No, just saw a clip from *Dirty Rotten Scoundrels*. Love that last scene."

Tim grabbed a Buzzard's Bay Lager from the fridge and handed it to him. "I'll be right out."

Hair wet, he reappeared dressed in T-shirt and clean jeans. His father had barely touched his beer and was in a leather recliner leafing through the latest *Sports Illustrated*. Tim got a beer and sat on the sofa opposite him. "Anything interesting?"

His father smiled. "Gonna be a great year for the Sox."

"Yup."

"I like your pad. Reminds me of my bachelor days."

Tim gave him a wry look. "Pad?"

"You know what I mean. The old bachelor pads."

"Which you would know little about since you grew up on a dairy farm in Vermont and never left home till you and Mom moved to the farm."

"You're forgettin' my four years at UVM. No fancy dorms then."

"Well, I'm a long way from college."

"You know, we have over a hundred acres. Plenty of it's not zoned for farming. We kept Land's End for you and your brothers and sisters."

"And it's beautiful, Dad, but I'm a single guy. Why would I want to build a house? I've got everything I need right here."

Rex's kind eyes regarded his son. "Don't you think that might change someday?"

Tim chuckled. "Not anytime soon."

"Gail's a great gal."

"Yes, she is."

"Must've been a shock for her. The business this morning."

Tim shook his head. "How does news travel so fast around here? I barely found out myself."

"I believe your sister saw Bobby Moniz in town. She told your mother, who came flying out to the east pasture on one of the golf carts to find me."

Tim leaned back, smiling. "So you came flying into town."

"Somethin' like that. So what's up with the Hodge girl?"

"Well, for one thing, she's far from a girl anymore."

"Still pretty messed up, I hear."

"Yup."

"I'm sorry, son."

Tears rimmed his eyes as Tim turned to his father. "It was awful, Dad."

"I can only imagine."

"I mean, I'm over Izzy. I don't... I mean I don't imagine a life with her anymore. That's history. But seeing her so messed up, so frail and broken. It was horrible."

"Where is she now?"

"I haven't got a clue. I'm going to the station and see if they'll let me talk to the guy she was with. See if he'll tell me where she might've gone."

"Is that wise?"

"I have to try. She has no one. No family, siblings, no one. If I don't at least try, she's going to die. I can't let that happen."

"What about Gail?"

"What would she possibly want with a loser like me?"

"Now *that's* messed up," Rex said, setting his beer down. "If she cares about you, she's your soft place, son. She and Coop and your family."

"I like Gail, a lot, but I can't drag her into this."

"Sounds like you already did. What did she say about this morning?"

"I haven't talked to her."

"Why not?"

"Look, Dad, I've got to take care of this first. Clear my head, you know? One thing at a time."

"You owe her an explanation."

"I know, I know... When I get back from the station, I'll call her."

"I'll drive you. Come on."

Knowing it was useless to argue with his father, the stubbornest person he knew, Tim grabbed keys and his jacket. "Come on, then. Let's do this."

CHAPTER 24

"You can't see him, and that's that," Pete Avery said.

"Did he tell you where she is?" Tim said.

Pete shook his head. "I shouldn't tell you a thing, but no. He's told us shit except to complain about the food. We've traced some of the stuff in the truck to things people reported missing in Bayport. Apparently, that's where they were last week. We can't keep him here. He's being transferred to the county jail in the morning."

"Please, just five minutes," Tim said.

"Go home Tim. Let us handle this."

Rex nodded to Avery, hand on Tim's shoulder. "Come on, son."

Tim shrugged out of his grasp. "This is bullshit."

"No, it's the law. Now go home."

Tim slammed out of the station and headed for his father's truck. When he reached it, he pounded on the side of the truck with a closed fist.

"You dent my truck, you fix it. Now watch out before you break a bone. Then where would you be?"

Ignoring him, Tim got into the passenger seat. "Now where do we go?"

Rex slid in. "Nowhere. You're going to go home and let it go. Let her go."

"I can't, Dad. Not till I know she's okay."

"Even if she's never gonna be okay?"

"Even then."

"Well, there's always Frankie," Rex said, referring to one of his wife's friends and a member of the Darn Yarners. Among her many jobs, Frankie worked as a private investigator. Most of her work was insurance fraud and the occasional trailing of an errant spouse, but she had worked on a couple of missing persons cases over the years.

Tim let out a long deep breath. "Think she'd do it?"

"Maybe. Even though it's against my better judgment, I'd say you could ask her."

"Think she'd be home?"

"Only one way to find out." Rex turned the truck out of the station lot and headed south onto Beach Street, the road that ran along the lower peninsula. It was lined with small beach cottages on both sides. Frankie lived on the water side, in a shingled boathouse on stilts. Half of the two-story dwelling was over the water, a long dock stretching out into the river. One expected to see a hobbit emerge from the carved front door rounded at the top.

She answered the door in overalls covered with paint splotches, her wiry salt-and-pepper curls held back by a faded bandana the same blue as her sharp eyes. Tall and slender, she was a strong, lithe fifty-eight years old. "Hi, guys. This is a surprise. Is this a social call?"

"Sort of," Rex said, kissing her cheek. "Have you got a few minutes?"

"For two gorgeous men? What do you think? Come on back. Just finishing a project."

They followed her through the rabbit warren of rooms onto the deck. "Something to drink? Beer? Lemonade? Water?"

"I'm good, thanks, Frankie," Tim answered.

"Well, I'd love a lemonade," Rex said, settling down in one of several cushioned deck chairs.

"Good. I'll fix three," she said, disappearing.

"This place is amazing," Tim said. "How long has Frankie been here?"

"Since before your mom and I got married. It was an old shack when she first moved in. One of a kind now."

"What's that?" their hostess asked, stepping onto the deck, tray of glasses in hand. She set it down and handed each of them a frosted mug of lemonade. She'd also brought a plate of cookies.

"Thanks, darlin'. Never could resist your ginger cookies. We were talkin' about your one-of-a-kind house." Rex took two cookies and leaned back, a grin on his face.

She sat opposite father and son. "So, to what do I owe this pleasure?"

Tim cleared his throat, then launched into a brief description of the past few days, ending with "Can you help me find her? It's really important, Frankie."

For several minutes, Frankie sat watching boats coming in for the day, the river calm and peaceful after a breezy afternoon. Finally, she said, "Never knew the Hodge girl, except from your mom's accounts and seeing her with you around town. Are you sure you want to find her after all this time and in view of recent events?"

"I just want to know she's okay. Then I can leave it alone," Tim said.

"Sounds like she's clearly not okay," Frankie said.

Rex nodded. "Just what I said."

Tim set down his glass, ignoring his father. "I'll pay whatever you want. Please, Frankie."

"Why don't we do this. You give me everything you know. I'll try to get down to County and see her friend, this Ice person, even though they probably won't let me near him. I'll do a little digging, and if I incur costs, I'll let you know."

They talked a few minutes longer, sipping lemonade and watching the river, then father and son said goodbye. When Rex dropped Tim at his apartment, he said, "Get a good night's sleep and call your girl."

"Thanks, Dad. And tell Mom not to worry."

"Yeah, right. That would be after we watch the herd of pigs fly over the barn," Rex said, waving as he backed out.

CHAPTER 25

"It's real cute," Pam said as she and Gail climbed the rise to their mom's bench. It had become their afternoon ritual. The path was now lined with thousands of daffodils and grape hyacinths, a riot of spring color.

"I'm glad for you," Gail said, "even though I'll be sorry to see you go."

"Five minutes away, dearie. Besides, as I've told you since I got here, *you* can come too! The house has three bedrooms. Plenty of room."

"I could, couldn't I? I mean, they haven't said definitely, but I think Lucy intends to sell her house and move here. She'd probably be happy with fewer Morgans underfoot."

Pam paused on the path, looking over at her. "If Lucy sells her house, that means baby brother is displaced too. What's his plan?"

"Aside from the vintner's little house, there are two apartments above the main barn. Pretty nice ones, from what I've seen," Gail said. "Ravenstock's assistant is having one, so I guess Wolfie could take the other. Nothing's decided 'cause Wolfie hasn't given Dad a definite yes."

They reached the top of the hill, and Pam threw out her arms, turning her face upward to the sun. "What a beautiful place this is!"

"Yes," Gail said, following her gaze across the fields.

"You think Wolfie will like running a vineyard?" Pam flopped down on their mom's bench. "Or that he'll be any good at it?"

Gail laughed, sitting beside her. "Who knows? Dad thinks he's perfect, so if he isn't, he will be before Dad finishes with him. Wants to send him to a bunch of vineyards over the next few months, I guess to see how they do it."

"He's a funny one, our brother."

"We had lunch today. He was very supportive when I needed it."

"No word from Tim?"

"No, and I haven't even told you about my morning." She proceeded to relate the story again. The expression on Pam's face told her that the shocking tale was hitting its mark.

"Oh my goodness," Pam said. "What a god-awful mess. And he hasn't called?"

"Nope."

"Have you tried him?"

"Yup, many times."

Pam draped her arm around Gail's shoulders and hugged her. "Poor baby. You better move in with me."

Gail frowned. "If I lived in the village, I'd be bumping into him every other minute."

"Well then, how about this? I have some money saved, and I just decided last night that I'm going to travel before I look for a job around here. I can't move into the house for six weeks, so I thought I'd go somewhere. Haven't decided where yet. Want to come with me?"

Gail stared at her, marveling at her sister's blithe spirit. "I can't just go sailing off somewhere. Dad needs me."

"Bullshit. I mean, I know you do important work, dearie, but I guarantee Morgan Enterprises and Morgan's Fire can survive for a month without you."

Gail's cell buzzed, and she pulled it from her jacket pocket, spying Tim's name as caller. "It's him, excuse me."

She stood and walked a short distance away. "Hello?"

"Hey, sorry I've been out of touch."

"How are you?"

"More important, how are you?"

"Okay."

"I'm so sorry about this morning."

"Wasn't your fault."

"Still, you never should have been in the middle of it."

"So is everything all right?" she asked, not sure what to say next.

"I wondered if you wanted to get together tonight? I understand if you don't, but I'd like to see you…to tell you—"

"That would be fine," she said, interrupting him.

"My place? Or we could go out?"

"You place is fine. What time?"

"Would seven work for you?"

"Yes, fine. What's your address?"

He gave her the address, and they rang off.

When Gail returned to the bench, she felt numb.

"So?" Pam asked.

"So I'm going over to his place for dinner."

"That sounds nice."

"Maybe." Gail extended her hand to her sister. "Can we head back?"

"Fine with me. Guess it's just Weezie and me for supper, then."

"So where are you going on your trip?" Gail asked as they headed down the path.

"I don't know 'cause I just dreamed this up this morning. I could stay domestic and travel across the country, go to Hawaii or Alaska. I was also thinking about Canada. There's always the UK too. I'm dying to travel around England, Scotland, Wales, Ireland. You name it, I want to go there."

Gail smiled. "You've got some serious thinking to do. Won't it be tough making last-minute plans?"

"Not in today's world. After that river cruise I took with Aunt Cherie last year, I get emails about deals constantly. That's another idea—a river cruise anywhere. So cool!"

CHAPTER 26

Gail arrived at Tim's shortly after seven. The heady aroma of spices and garlic met her on the stairs. When he opened the door, she said, "Something smells good."

He smiled, and her heart melted. All thoughts of being cautious flew out the open window.

"I wish I could take credit. Got it all at the Grille. Hope you like eggplant parmesan?"

"Love it." She stood in the doorway, frozen to the spot.

"Great, come in," he said, leaning forward, kissing her cheek, then standing aside to allow her to pass.

What a difference. Less than forty-eight hours ago, there was such heat, such connection, and now that connection has vanished. "Great apartment," she said, gazing around at his comfortable, tasteful furnishings. He had a number of beautiful paintings, some abstracts, some landscapes, several depicting local scenes. He followed her gaze, then said, "My one indulgence. I love local art festivals and always come back with something. I'm gonna run out of wall space soon."

She smiled. "It's a lovely eclectic collection."

"Thanks. What can I get you to drink? I have beer, red or white wine, and stuff like seltzer and a few sodas."

"I'd love red wine, please."

He opened a bottle of Chianti and poured them each a glass. "Here, come sit."

Gail sat beside him on the comfortable couch, leaning back, sipping the delicious wine. "Life turns on a dime, doesn't it?" she asked.

"You can say that again. I'm really sorry about this morning."

"You've already said that."

"I know, but I feel like such a shit for putting you through that."

"You didn't. I was just in the wrong place at the wrong time."

"Because of me."

Gail set down her wine and reached across to touch his arm. "Don't beat yourself up. I'm a big girl. It's over, Coop handled it, and Mr. Ice is in custody."

He grinned. "Mr. Ice, that's a good one. I didn't even get to see the sleazeball she's been hangin' out with."

"You aren't missing much." *He looks tired*, she thought, dark circles under his beautiful dark eyes. She fingered the soft flannel of his shirt as she gently massaged his arm. *Arm's so tense, it feels like it could snap.*

"You know what I want right now?" His eyes left little doubt as to his thoughts.

She smiled. "I think I know, but why don't you tell me anyway?"

"You look pretty tonight. I love you in jeans."

"And this old sweatshirt?"

"Yup, but much as I love you in jeans and that sweatshirt, I'd love to get you out of them and into my arms so I can feel your incredible warm naked body against mine. Too bad I have no right to ask after all the shit I've put you through."

Gail stood, gazing down at him, eyes soft. "Well, if I'm going to get naked, don't you think you should too?" She pulled her sweatshirt and bra off with one motion, then unzipped her jeans.

Tim's jaw dropped as he watched her. Then he too stood up. "Okay, then," he said and threw off his clothes.

They stood facing each other, still not touching. "You are the most beautiful thing I've ever seen," he said, voice hoarse with desire.

"You're pretty beautiful yourself."

"Can I kiss you?"

"If you don't, I'm going to lose it." She reached out as he enveloped her in his arms, his heat igniting a flame deep in her belly.

His lips captured hers, and they pressed against one another, his cock already rock-hard against her body. He trailed kisses down her neck, then took one, then the other breast in his mouth, sucking and teasing her nipples to exquisite hardness. Gail arched into him, an agony of sensation washing over her as she slid her hand down to take him, stroking the way she already knew he loved it.

Then his fingers moved down between her legs, thumb pressed against the bundle of nerves at her clit, as he pushed two fingers deeper. That was enough, Gail lost it, screaming through something more powerful than she'd ever experienced. As she writhed in the aftershocks of her orgasm, she rubbed against him, crying, "More, more, more!"

In answer, he lifted her, carrying her into the bedroom, laying her on the bed. "More? What do you want, babe?"

"You. In me, please."

"Cock or tongue?"

Eyes wide, Gail met his gaze. "Cock?"

He opened the bedside table drawer and grabbed a condom, then slipped it on. "You ready, baby?"

Gail nodded, opening her legs. She couldn't talk. In fact, at the moment, she could

barely breathe. As he moved over her, Gail reached up, hands on his hard, taut belly as he wrapped her legs around him. With his first thrust, she felt her breath release and cried, "Oh!" the last coherent sound for many minutes as they moved in perfect synchrony to a smashing crescendo. Afterward, she lay limp in his arms, Tim trailing gentle kisses over her arms, neck, and shoulder.

"You hungry?" he said at last.

"Starved."

"Good. Maybe we'll save my tongue work for dessert?"

"Something to look forward to," she whispered, kissing him deeply, her tongue curling around his.

"Come on," he said, "or we'll start something before dinner that we can't stop."

"Is that a bad thing?"

He grinned. "No, you wicked woman, but I want to feed you. You're starving, remember?"

They padded into the living room and pulled on clothes. Gail stuck her panties in her purse. *They'll be off again in an hour or so.* "Can I help?" she asked, hugging him from behind as he stood at the stove.

"There's dressing there," he said, pointing to the counter. "You can toss the salad."

CHAPTER 27

"This is incredible," she said, popping another bite of eggplant into her mouth.

"Rosa and Cesar know how to make a great parm," he said. "So I figure, why bother trying. I could never come close to this."

They ate in silence for a few minutes until Gail pointed toward the bedroom and said, "So that was a surprise. A happy one, but not what I expected."

"Good. It was good," he said, setting down his fork. "Probably selfish of me, but amazing."

"Why selfish? We both wanted it."

"Yes, but my life's complicated right now, and that... This isn't fair to you."

Gail's heart sank as she stared at him, afraid to hear his next words. "What do you mean?"

"I mean, I've got to find her, make sure she's okay, hopefully get her into rehab."

"Then what?"

"Then I don't know. If she's able to be on her own, great."

"And if not?" Gail felt anger bubbling up, anger to push away the hurt.

"I care deeply for you, Gail. I don't want to lose you, but I'm all Izzy has. She has no family left."

"Is that how you see your relationship, family?"

"No, but I feel like if I can help I should, you know?"

Gail fought hard for composure. *Don't cry! See this through.* "Where does that leave us?"

"I honestly don't know. I wish I could say more."

"How do you propose to find her?"

"I've hired a private investigator."

"When?"

"Today, this afternoon."

Shocked, she stared at him, the warm glow of their lovemaking a distant memory, her heart as cold as ice. "You were able to find someone that quickly?"

"It's my mom's friend, Frankie Brown. She lives—"

"Right next door to my sister Pam's rental."

"Really?"

"She just signed the lease today."

"Frankie's great. Not sure she'll have any luck, but I had to try."

Gail took a gulp of wine, setting down her glass with a thud. "So what's this all been?" She waved her hand back and forth between them. "Have I just been a distraction while you waited for Izzy to return?"

"No, of course not. You… This has been amazing. The best thing that's ever happened to me. I care for you, Gail. I think there's a part of me that's in love with you."

"The horny part?" she said, instantly regretting her words. *This isn't me. Don't go there! Don't lose control.*

"Absolutely not! Don't get me wrong, the sex has been extraordinary, but I'm talking about my feelings for you, not sex."

Gail shook her head. "I'm sorry, I'm just not understanding, I guess. Are you with me or Izzy?"

"You, but I have to find her…to make sure she's all right."

"The woman I saw this morning is clearly *not* all right."

"No, but if I can help her, then—"

"Then what?"

"Then we can see. Please try to understand. This time with you has been some of the happiest of my life and I don't want to lose you, but she's part of me. Part of my soul. I just can't turn away."

Gail felt as if he'd kicked her in the chest. *Part of my soul? What the hell am I doing here?* She pushed back from the table and stood. "I've gotta go."

"Wait Gail, please."

"No! This is over. You need to find your soul mate and leave me alone."

She grabbed her bag, flung open the door, and ran down the stairs. Tears blurred her eyes as she raced to her car. "Gail, wait!" he called, but she ignored him, hopping in and locking the door.

He reached the car and tapped on the window.

She put her hand on the glass. "No!" Then she turned on the ignition and backed away, refusing to look at him. As she rounded the corner, she gazed back in the rearview mirror and saw him standing in the lot, hands on hips. *Goodbye, Tim Miller. What a silly fool I've been!*

Pam called from the dining room as she came in. "Hey, sis, we're back here!"

"I can't," Gail said, choking on her tears.

Her sister appeared almost instantly. "Oh geez, what happened?"

"It's over. Finished. Kaput!" Gail said, collapsing in her sister's arms.

Weezie joined them in the hall. "Looks like we need some of Dad's single malt Scotch and we need it now!"

CHAPTER 28

Tim sat at his parents' kitchen table, drinking coffee. After fifteen minutes of hovering, his mom had left the room. He pulled out his cell and tried Gail for what seemed like the hundredth time. And for the hundredth time, it went straight to voicemail.

Faith Miller peeked her head around the door to the laundry room. "Leave her alone, honey. She deserves that."

"I've gotta go, Mom. Thanks for breakfast."

"Anytime!" she called as he banged out the screen door.

He spied his father stepping out of his truck, laden with bags. "Hey, son! Been in town. Sorry I missed you."

Tim raised his hand to shield his eyes from the bright morning sun. "I was looking through a box of papers in my old room. Mom made me breakfast."

"And gave you a shitload of unsolicited advice, I'll wager."

Tim smiled. "Breakfast was great."

"Where you off to?"

"I'm pulling pots this morning, then I'll be in the workshop all afternoon. You guys want lobsters? I forgot to ask Mom."

"Only if you have plenty. And we'll pay market price."

"Miller market price," he said, the familiar conversation playing out.

"Any word from Frankie?"

"Nope. I thought I'd check in after work."

"She'll call if she has news, I expect. What about your girl? How's she doing?"

"Don't know. Gail won't speak to me."

"Uh-oh."

"My fault. I don't blame her. Who wants to be part of a three-person relationship where one party is a ghost?"

"Give it time, son."

"See ya, Dad."

As he drove away, Tim gazed out at the acres of fields and woods. Countless times in high school and college, he had fantasized about building a house for Izzy at the edge of the woods facing the bay. He thought back to the girl and woman he'd known and loved. Izzy had had an infectious laugh and a blithe spirit that found wonder and joy in almost anything. Before the drugs, she would have delighted in planning a home together. A home set in the woods where they loved to hike and camp. Tim's heart ached with sadness as he remembered nights under the stars, the two of them lying side by side on old camp blankets.

*****

Gail found Pam in her pajamas at the kitchen table, eating toast, laptop open. "Okay, I'm in."

"Excuse me?" her sister said, looking up over her reading glasses. Gail was fully dressed, neat as a pin as always in pressed khakis and a pale blue cotton sweater, a brightly patterned infinity scarf around her neck.

"Are you researching for your trip?"

"No, job hunting. I want to get things set up before I go. Those colors suit you. You should wear blues and greens more often."

"Thanks. This is J. Jill," she said fingering the scarf.

"Hey sis, what did you mean, you're in?"

"I want to go on the trip with you. I don't care where. I just want to get away."

"I'm leaning toward the UK. I really want to go to Cornwall to Port Isaac."

"Home of Doc Martin! I love that show. I'd definitely do that."

"Then, I was thinking Wales. There are great hikes in Wales. But really, anywhere is fine. We could rent a car and just go. Maybe spend a few days or a week in London at some point, but otherwise just go where the spirit moves us."

"That sounds perfect. We could even go up to Scotland or fly to Ireland?"

"Soon as I write this email to the schools, I'll switch gears and look for flights. I was thinking of taking off the day Dad and Lucy get home."

"Could we wait at least a day in case he has stuff for me to do before I go?" Gail said.

"Absolutely!" Pam raised her hand for a high five, and Gail responded.

"Thanks, sis, this is just what I need right now."

"Me too," Pam said. "It's gonna be cool."

CHAPTER 29

The week flew by with preparations for the trip and her work for the farm and vineyard. Gail knew her father would wholeheartedly support her going, but she hated to leave him in the lurch. Promotion and fundraising efforts for the mustang rescue were all planned for midsummer, and the vineyard advertising wasn't slated to kick into high gear until fall or winter. Truth was, Rich ran the business, Weezie helped at the stables, and her work was more of a hobby. *Maybe when I return, I'll look for a real job*, Gail thought as she drove into town.

She was just exiting Averill's General Store when she spied Tim walking up the sidewalk toward her. He was looking down and hadn't seen her, but there was no way to avoid him. Her car was in the lot just behind him. As she steeled herself, he looked up, his gorgeous dark eyes registering surprise. More drawn and tired than he'd been the last time she saw him, Gail's heart went out to the man she loved. *There, I've said it, and a lot of good it does me!* This thought gave her courage as she neared him.

"Hey," he said, stopping.

"Hey." She gazed down at the sidewalk unable to meet his eyes.

"I've been trying to reach you."

"No point, really."

"Well, I disagree. I'm pretty sure I botched things the other night, and I want to apologize."

"Are you still looking for her?"

"Yes, but—"

"Then I can't. I'm sorry," Gail said.

"It's not what you think."

"Does it matter?"

He reached out, attempting to take her hand, but she jumped back. "To me it does. Listen, I've got frozen stuff in these bags, so I've got to get going."

"Can I see you?"

"Not right now. Maybe someday."

"Can I call you?"

"What good would it do? You take care of whatever you have to do and don't worry about me."

"Gail, please," he said, but she was already walking away, fighting back tears as she hurried to her car.

"Hey, Tim, how're ya doin'?" a voice called behind him. It was Kyle Morgan, Gail's cousin and the village veterinarian.

"Hey, Kyle. Doing fine. You?" Tim straightened up, endeavoring to shake off the sadness of his encounter with Gail.

"Never better, but you don't look so fine, man. You sure you're okay?"

"Good as I can be."

"Woman trouble, huh?"

Tim smiled at the dark-haired vet. He liked Kyle, and his arrival had been a godsend to local farmers and pet owners. "Something like that."

"Buy you a cup of coffee?"

"Thanks, but I gotta be somewhere."

"So the honeymooners come back tomorrow, I hear."

"Yeah?"

"Yup, and if Harriet hears good things about the Seychelles from her sister, I bet the pressure'll be on for us to go there next winter."

"That's right. You guys aren't married yet?"

Kyle laughed. "Nope, just seems like we are. Well, I'll let you go, man. Have a good one."

"You too." Tim headed for his workshop. *What will Richard Morgan think when he hears I've broken his daughter's heart?*

His cell buzzed, and he pulled it from his pocket. He didn't recognize the number, but said, "Hello?"

"Tim, this is Frankie Brown. I found her."

*****

Rich and Weezie were already at the dining room table when Gail returned. Pam's car was gone. "Hey, sis, did you forget?" Weezie called.

"Weekly meeting?" Rich waved a file at her as Gail set groceries on the counter.

"Shit, sorry. Totally slipped my mind. Let me throw the cold stuff in the fridge, and I'll be right in."

An hour later, they'd gone through the usual list of business tasks when Pam banged in the back door. Callie poked her head into the dining room. "Anyone want lunch? I'm making chicken salad."

They all asked for sandwiches, and Pam poured everyone iced tea. As they dove into thick, delicious sandwiches, Weezie said, "Too bad we didn't get Wolfie over here. Ava too."

"Maybe the night after Dad and Lucy get home," Gail said. "Be nice to have a family dinner before Pam and I take off."

"I'm so jealous," Weezie said. "Maybe I'll come join you for a week in the middle."

"There's room in the car," Pam said. "God I love Callie's chicken salad. Thanks, Cal!" she called toward the kitchen.

"So you gonna be okay, sis?" Rich asked, turning to Gail.

It was rare, if ever, that their oldest sibling talked about feelings, so Gail stared at him for a few seconds before answering. "Yup. Right as rain."

"Why don't we believe you?" Weezie said.

Pam frowned at her. "Drop it, both of you."

Gail raised her hands. "No, no, it's fine. I'm fine. Tim and I broke up, it was really hard, but I'm putting the pieces back together. Fortunately, we weren't together long. Not like recovering from a thirty-year marriage breakup. And," she turned to Pam, "this trip will help move me forward. Can't wait."

"Well, I'm glad you're going," Rich said. "Have you told Dad?"

"He's on his honeymoon. I'll tell him tonight. My guess is with his new bride and settling in here, not to mention moving out of Lucy's house, that he won't even notice I'm gone."

"Are her kids moving in here?" Pam asked.

"That's the plan," Gail said. "We have eight bedrooms in this behemoth of a house. Had to be some reason Dad built it so big."

"Big or not, it'll be an adjustment for everyone," Pam said.

Gail nodded. "Fortunately, we have a big table."

"Newlyweds living like *The Brady Bunch*? Yikes!" Pam said.

"Well, I'm outta here," their brother said. "See everyone tonight." He was picking their father and Lucy up in Boston.

"Safe trip," Gail said, nibbling on one of Callie's homemade potato chips.

CHAPTER 30

Tim met Frankie in the Emergency Room at Saint Anne's Hospital in Fall River, about a thirty-minute drive from the village. "She's in pretty rough shape. They've patched her up, but they can't keep her long."

He followed her to one of the curtained cubicles, the occupant of the bed almost unrecognizable. Her clothes were splattered with blood, her eyes were blackened and swollen shut. A six-inch gash on her forehead had been stitched, her mouth was three times its normal size, and her left arm was in a cast.

The attending physician stood beside the bed. As he turned to them, he brushed sandy blond hair from his forehead. "Broken arm, three broken ribs, maybe some internal bleeding. At least with the cast, there's one fewer place she can shoot up."

Tim wondered if the man standing in front of him might be crazy. "And you're discharging her?"

"We can't keep her. She wants to go. I gave her a prescription for methadone. Should get her through the next few days, but that's pretty much all I can do unless she agrees to rehab."

"She's also a wanted felon," Frankie said, raising her hand as Tim started to protest. "Not for your robbery. She and her friend have been linked to a number of recent robberies."

"Cops should be here soon," the doctor said. "They had another guy to take care of first."

When the physician disappeared, Tim sat by the bedside and took her right hand. "Hey, Iz, it's me."

She turned her head toward the opposite wall. "Go away, Tim. Please," she said, voice muffled through swollen lips.

"No."

She closed her eyes. "I need to sleep."

Tim and Frankie stepped out into the ER lobby. He asked, "What happened? Do you know?"

Frankie shook her head. "I traced her to an abandoned building where she and that Ice person sometimes sleep. Found her in the second-floor stairwell. From what I can gather, she and her friend owe money, quite a lot of money, to a dealer. I guess he got tired of waiting. Honestly, I think she's a small fish. They want Ice, but they beat her up as a warning. If he doesn't come through, next time she'll be dead."

"He's in jail. How can he help?"

"He was released four days ago."

"That's it, then. She's going to rehab."

"You may not have that choice," Frankie said, gazing down the hall behind him.

Two police officers approached. They stopped a nurse, and Tim heard one of them say, "We're here to pick up the Hodge woman."

"Wait!" he called, waving his hand at them.

"Who are you?" one of the officers said.

"Tim Miller, a friend."

"Sorry, Mr. Miller, you have no standing here."

"She needs rehab, not jail. Please, can't you wait for me to make a couple of calls?"

"Nope. We've got to process her. Rehab would be a judge's call. Now excuse me."

Tim tried to bar the door, but Frankie pulled him back, and the two officers pushed by.

A moment later, they reappeared with Izzy between them. Their firm grasp on her arms seemed to be the only thing keeping her from the floor.

"Iz, I'll be there soon!" he said.

"Leave me alone!" she snapped. "Leave me the fuck alone."

Frankie took hold of his arm. "Come on. Nothing you can do now. She'll be locked up here in town for at least a day."

Tears in his eyes, he allowed himself to be dragged to the parking lot. Numb, he sat in his truck, staring straight ahead. Frankie came around and sat beside him. "Can I give you some words of advice?"

He shrugged. "Do I have a choice?"

"Let the system take it from here. When she's served her time, maybe then she'd consent to rehab."

"She is a cop. She won't last six months in jail."

"*Was* a cop," Frankie said.

"Doesn't matter. From what I hear, word travels fast when you're incarcerated in a state facility."

"The only other option would be to get her a good lawyer who can argue for rehab rather than jail. It's a long shot, though. She's got a bunch of outstanding warrants."

"For?"

"Theft, prostitution, drugs. She's had a rough ten years."

Tim slumped down, head on the steering wheel. "Okay then, I'll call Raffi. See who he recommends for a criminal attorney." He referred to his childhood friend, Raphael Rodriguez, an environmental lawyer.

CHAPTER 31

"England? And you're leaving tomorrow?" Richard gazed from one daughter to the other. "Lucy and I just got back."

"Exactly," Gail said. "Pam and I thought it would be great for you to have the house to yourself."

"Except for Weezie, Amy, and Rob," he said. "This seems kind of sudden."

Pam gazed at her sister, then him. "It's my idea. I want to travel a bit before getting a job, and I can't move into my house for six weeks."

"Where is Lucy anyway?" Gail asked.

"We dropped her at her house to see the kids and get organized. They're not planning to move in for a bit. There's so much to get settled."

"What's happening to her house anyway?" Pam asked.

"I believe her ex-husband's taking it over. It was his family home."

Gail looked at him. "So Lucy doesn't own it?"

"She owns a share. It's kind of a weird arrangement. Apparently, he has to buy her out," Richard said. "It's her business, so I haven't gotten into it."

"Good thing you built this big house. What rooms are the kids taking?" Pam asked.

"She's bringing them over sometime soon so they can choose," he said.

Their Maine house had had seven bedrooms. Richard liked to say he'd learned from that project. This rambling farmhouse had nine bedrooms including the third-floor loft. The master suite was on the first floor behind his office, with French doors that led to a private terrace. Callie's bedroom and bath were behind the kitchen and the second floor had six bedrooms, all with their own bath. The loft space also had a small bathroom under the eaves.

"I vote we keep the loft for a guestroom. It's a cool space," Gail said.

"Maybe," he said. "But I want Lucy's kids to have their pick, and if one of 'em loves the loft, it's theirs."

"Think it'll be weird for them to move out of town to way out here?" Pam asked.

"Maybe. This isn't the wilderness, though. Rob gets his license soon, so that'll help," her father said. "I've asked Callie to make us a special dinner tonight. Good thing too, if you guys are abandoning us in the morning. What's new, anyway?"

"Not much," Gail said. "I've left a bunch of paperwork for you to go through. Publicity for the vineyard is all set, and I've explained everything to Rich."

"I wasn't asking about the business," he said. "How are things with your handsome woodworker?"

Gail crossed her arms. "They're not. His old girlfriend came back, and he's with her now."

Her sister and Richard exchanged looks, then Pam said, "Well, that's not technically true. He's not *with* her, he's helping her. Two different things."

"Well, no matter what, I don't want to be in the middle of it."

Richard looked from one daughter to the other, his expression puzzled. "In the middle of what?"

Gail threw up her hands. "Who knows?"

"You might know if you answered just one of his calls," Pam snapped.

The two sisters, mostly Gail, gave their father a quick summary of the events of the past weeks, with Izzy's return, the robbery and all. Pam ended with, "Last thing I heard was that Frankie Brown, Lucy's mom's detective friend, was helping Tim locate Izzy."

"Frankie's a private investigator," he said.

Gail stared at her sister. "Who told you that?"

"Frankie lives next to the house I'm renting, and another neighbor told me," Pam said.

"When?" Gail asked.

"Hold on, hold on. I just heard it this morning. I was going to tell you when Dad drove in."

"Well, if you want my two cents—" Richard said.

Gail stood up. "I don't! I've got packing to do."

"Call him!" her father cried as she headed out of the kitchen.

*****

Coop watched his friend return his cell phone to his pocket for the tenth time that morning. "Put yourself out of your misery and go to her house."

"What the hell are you talking about?" Tim said.

"Like I don't know who you've been calling all morning? Come on, buddy. I've known you for thirty-six years."

"Leave it, Coop."

"Okay, but Gail Morgan is your present and Izzy is your past. Time to step up and tell the woman how you feel about her."

"Once things are settled with Iz, maybe."

"Maybe nothing. I've seen the way you look at her, man. Haven't seen that *ever,* even in the Izzy years."

Tim shrugged. "Maybe I'll go out to the farm in a day or two, but right now, I've got a shitload of work to do."

He turned his back on Coop and with a heavy heart resumed work on a maple dining room table. The piece was near to completion except for the finishing, which took over a week. The owners had also commissioned eight chairs, but the preliminary work was completed by a fellow woodworker, then brought to Tim for final finishing. It felt good to work, his frayed nerves soothed by the manual labor. As he moved the sander slowly back and forth on the grain, he thought about Gail and his feelings for her.

This relationship was so different than it had been with Izzy, even in the early years. Izzy and he had grown up together and were like two peas in a pod. That was before separation and the strain of her job began to pull them apart, the peas scattering to the four corners of the earth. In many ways, Izzy had been like a sister. There had, of course, been a fierce attraction, fueled by raging adolescent hormones. He and Izzy had learned about sex together.

Now Gail kindled a fire deep in his belly, a craving and longing to connect on levels he never knew existed. He missed her terribly, her sweet smile, her kindness, her gentle, self-effacing personality that he found so endearing. He missed her warmth, her beautiful body that fit his so perfectly. Izzy was a part of his soul, like the memories of his youth, but Gail had pierced that soul, and she was his future. He was certain of that. *I'll just get Izzy back on her feet, then I can give Gail what she so richly deserves. I'll find her tomorrow and tell her. Maybe she'll understand and give me a second chance.*

CHAPTER 32

As Richard and Lucy drove Pam and Gail to the airport in Boston, she turned to smile at the sisters sitting side by side in the backseat. "I'm so jealous. After our beautiful trip to the Seychelles, I've caught the travel bug. I'd love to be driving around England. So many wonderful places to see."

"Have you spent much time there?" Pam asked.

"Only a few days in London many years ago," Lucy said. "We drove out to Stonehenge, but that's it except the city, and there's so much to see in London, we barely scratched the surface."

"We're there a week," Pam said, "but we could always loop back if we want. We have a completely open itinerary except for our hotel reservations in London."

"Well, enjoy every minute," Richard said. "You were too young to remember the month we spent in England before moving back to the States."

Gail gazed out the window and thought about Tim and how far away he would be. Even though she wasn't answering his calls, she found herself anticipating them and was sad when they had ceased the previous morning. *Let it go,* she reminded herself. *No sense in dwelling. Use this trip to heal and let go.*

As if reading her mind, Lucy said, "Not to bring up a painful subject, but I was sorry to hear about you and Tim. Does he know you're leaving?"

Gail shook her head. "Haven't talked to him in days."

"He's been calling nonstop," Pam said.

"Not anymore," Gail replied. "Guess he's given up."

"Well, I haven't," her father said. "I still think there's hope once he gets that friend of his settled."

"Well, you're the only one," Gail said, gazing out the window again.

"No, he isn't," Pam said. "I think there's hope, and I'll bet Lucy and anyone else who's seen you together does too."

Lucy reached back and patted Gail's knee. "Time for all that next month. Some distance and space may work wonders. Let's hear more about your incredible itinerary."

Saying a silent prayer of thanks to her new stepmother, Gail smiled. "Yes, let's! I'm so excited to visit the Tate Modern. I've heard it's amazing."

"And the Tate Britain," Pam said. "There's also the National Gallery."

Their father nodded. "My favorite art gallery in London is the National Portrait Gallery, just off Leicester Square. Highly recommend it. While you're in that area, you can pick up some theater tickets at the discount ticket booth."

"I've got a list of the plays I'd love to see," Gail said. "Not sure we'll be able to do it all in seven days."

"We can always go back," her sister said.

Their lively conversation continued until they dropped them at Logan Airport. As they headed through security, Gail checked her phone. No missed calls, texts, or messages. *Time to* unplug, she thought, switching it off. They had both signed up for international calling plans, but Gail intended to use her phone for local calls as they navigated the UK. *Not for tortured conversations from across the sea.*

*****

After leaving Pam and Gail at the airport, Lucy and Richard made several trips back and forth from Lucy's house with boxes of her belongings. She planned to bring Amy and Rob over the following day to choose their rooms. Once that decision was made, they would make any necessary changes to the rooms according to her kids' wishes. She wasn't planning to move them or herself until they settled things on her house. Work completed, the newlyweds were sitting on the porch enjoying a glass of wine in the late afternoon.

Lucy sighed. "What a lovely night. It's so peaceful here."

"Can't wait till you're here permanently, my love," he said, reaching over to squeeze her hand.

"I'm afraid that won't be quite so peaceful. Living with teenagers rarely is."

"I'll love it. Besides, I'm used to it. Weezie's still an adolescent. Probably always will be."

Lucy smiled, gazing over at him. "I hope everyone will get along. I'm feeling especially guilty about displacing Wolfie."

"Don't. His apartment above the vineyard barn's gonna be cool, and it's a mile from here, so he'll have plenty of space."

"So he's given you his answer, then?" she said.

"Tomorrow. He asked for an extension. I don't think it's cold feet. He just wants to be sure."

"I don't blame him." Lucy gazed out at a truck coming up the drive. "Who's that?"

Richard stood up. "Looks like Tim's truck. Oh boy, I wonder if Gail told him she was leaving. Nothing I hate worse than being the bearer of bad news." He waved as Tim pulled up and hopped out.

The couple came down off the porch to meet him.

"Hi, Tim. So good to see you," Lucy said, hugging him.

"Hey, Mrs. Morgan?" Tim said, looking from one to the other. "Did I get that right?"

Lucy smiled, taking Richard's arm. "You did. It is indeed Mrs. Morgan, but with friends, it will always be Lucy."

Richard extended his hand, which Tim grasped firmly. "Hey, son, good to see you."

"How was the honeymoon?"

"Heaven," Richard replied. "Want to join us on the porch for a drink? We're enjoying the end of this spectacular day."

"Thanks that's very kind of you, but I'm actually looking for Gail. Is she here?"

Richard regarded him with sad eyes. "Son, you'd better come sit down, drink or no drink."

Tim complied, following them onto the porch and taking a seat opposite them. "Is she okay?" he asked, eyes betraying his distress.

Richard raised his hands. "Yes, yes, no worries. She's fine. Sure we can't get you a drink?"

"No, thanks."

The older man cleared his throat. "The truth is, she's gone. On an extended trip with her sister Pam."

Tim stood, pacing back and forth. "Where? For how long?"

"We were shocked too," Richard said. "They've gone to the UK. Trip's open-ended, but I believe they're intending to stay at least a month, maybe a bit longer."

"I don't believe it," Tim blurted. "Why?"

Richard regarded him with kind eyes. "Why don't I get you a beer or something stronger?"

"No, thanks, really. I'm sorry. I have no right to ask after the way I've treated her."

Lucy, who had observed the conversation quietly up to this point, said, "Of course you do. You care about Gail."

"And she, you," Richard said. "She just needed time and to get away. She and her sister haven't spent much time together in a number of years. It was Pam's idea. Gail just decided to go along. Fortunately, her passport was up-to-date."

"Well, thanks, then. I'll let you get back to enjoying your evening."

"Don't go," Lucy said.

"You both must think I'm a world-class shit, excuse my language."

"Not at all," Richard said. "You're helping an old friend. That's a kindness, and I'm certain Gail understands that. She's always been my organized, black-and-white child. She likes things neat and tidy and we all know love is messy. Give her time."

"Thanks, Richard, Lucy," Tim said, turning to go.

Richard and Lucy walked him to the truck. "If she's in contact, I'll let her know you stopped by," Richard said.

Tim nodded, then hopped into the truck.

"Take care, son," Richard called as Tim backed out.

"Poor guy," Lucy said as they walked arm in arm to the porch.

"The very definition of stuck between a rock and a hard place," her husband said.

Lucy nodded. "The picture looks grim for Izzy Hodge, the woman he's trying to help."

"Terrible disease, addiction."

"Especially so in her case, since she became addicted just doing her job."

Richard turned and kissed her temple. "We not in the paradise of the Seychelles anymore, but let's take Tim's advice and enjoy this beautiful evening. What do you say?"

"Yes, dear husband. I'd like that very much."

CHAPTER 33

Pam frowned at her sister. "You know if you mope about anymore, I'm going to explore London by myself."

They were having high tea at Marks and Spencer, and Gail had barely touched the food. Her conversation thus far had been monosyllables. "I wish Dad hadn't told me he came by the farm."

"What does it matter? You're not speaking to him anyway."

"It rattled me, that's all."

"I can see that, but we're in London. *London!* Arguably one of greatest cities in the world. That long face is really dragging me down."

Gail forced a smile. "I'm sorry. I'll be better with a good night's sleep. What's on the agenda for tomorrow?"

"Anything we want, but I was thinking a gallery or two, then a play at night? We could go to Leicester Square, grab some good tickets, then tour the National Portrait Gallery. Then we could have lunch and visit one of the Tates or whatever. Or we could be real tourists and take a bus tour, ride on the London Eye or go to the Tower."

Gail laughed. "We *are* real tourists!"

"Yes, but we don't want people to know that." Pam popped the remains of her watercress sandwich into her mouth.

"My dear sister, we stick out like sore thumbs, and everything about us screams American," Gail said.

"Speak for yourself. I'm fluent in French. Maybe I'll start speaking more French than English. That will fool 'em."

"Good luck with that!" Gail sipped her tea, smiling at her sister. *Coming on this trip is the best thing I could have done for myself. I'm with my dear sister, and we're seeing amazing sights. No more moping!*

*****

Several weeks passed, and Izzy's lawyer successfully argued for a stint in rehab rather than jail time. The judge agreed with many stipulations, including a thousand hours of community service once she completed rehab. Izzy was also ordered to have weekly drug tests and check-ins with her parole officer. Any deviation and she would be incarcerated for a minimum of eight years on the drug and robbery charges.

Frankie and the attorney accompanied Izzy to the rehabilitation facility. Izzy requested that Tim stay away. Reluctantly, he had acquiesced. He spent the day feverishly working on projects, and late in the afternoon, he trolled the river, pulling his lobster pots and checking the poachers' traps for crabs. In early evening, he returned to his apartment and showered. He had just grabbed a beer when the phone rang.

"Hi, Tim, it's Frankie."

"Hey, how'd it go?"

"Smooth. She's there, settled in," Frankie said.

"How was she?"

"Shaky, but she walked in under her own steam."

"Thanks, Frankie. Let me know what I owe you."

"Get some rest. She's in good hands."

Frankie rang off, and Tim leaned back in his recliner. His thoughts were not about Izzy, but the beautiful, extraordinary woman he had driven away. *Now she's across the ocean as far away from me as she can get. Don't blame her one bit.*

He heard the knock at his door and remembered that he'd agreed to have dinner with his sister Karen. "Hey, sis," he said, standing aside as she came in.

"You look like shit, big brother."

"Perfect. I feel like shit, so I might as well look the part."

Karen frowned at him. "Self-pity doesn't suit you, bro. Grab your jacket and let's go. I'm craving Cesar's clams linguini."

Settled into a booth at the Cove Grille on Main Street, brother and sister were greeted by owner Rosa Rodriquez, one of their parents' dear friends. Rosa was a Darn Yarner and also Karen's godmother. "Hey, kids, has Carla been over yet?"

"Yup," Karen said, "and here she comes with our drinks."

"On the house," the plump owner said. Even at sixty-seven, Rosa's hair was a lustrous dark brown, not a strand of gray. Cesar, her husband, although robust, looked more like her father than her husband. Her violet eyes sparkled as she gazed down at them, hands on hips. "Well, enjoy," she said, bustling off toward the kitchen.

Carla set down Karen's Chianti and his beer, took their orders, and disappeared.

"How's Iz?" Karen asked. At one time, she and Izzy had been friends along with Lucy's sister Harriet. The group had drifted apart when Izzy went to the academy.

Tim shrugged. "Your guess is as good as mine. At her request, I'm keeping my distance."

Karen sipped her wine, studying him. Finally, she said, "Don't you think that's for the best? I mean, you're not considering getting back together, are you?"

He shook his head. "Not likely."

"Not likely, but not impossible? Are you insane?"

"Don't you start too." He took a huge gulp of Coastal Lager, a product of a microbrewery in Southport.

"What about Gail?"

"There is no Gail. She won't speak to me, and now she's in England for at least a month, maybe longer."

"Really?" Karen said.

"Yup."

"That was kind of sudden, wasn't it?"

"Yup."

"Did she go on her own?"

Tim shook his head. "She's traveling with her sister Pam. The one who's just moved down from Maine."

"Must be nice, picking up and taking a cool trip like that on the spur of the moment."

"Can we change the subject, please?"

"Not yet. I want to hear what happened to you guys."

"Why, so you can run home and tell everyone?"

"Don't be ridiculous. I want to help."

"Well, you can't."

"I'm a woman. I might understand if you'd give me a try."

Tim caught Carla's eye and signaled for another beer. "What the hell." He proceeded to give Karen a brief summary of the past few weeks and his interactions with Gail.

When he stopped, Karen said, "Geez, that must have been creepy for Gail to meet Izzy that way."

"To say the least. It was a frickin' nightmare."

"I'm sorry. I bet with time she'll come around."

"I don't want her to come around. She deserves much better than me."

Karen frowned. "Bullshit. That's another quality that doesn't suit you—martrydom."

Carla appeared at that moment with huge platters of food. Tim smiled up at her. "Thanks, Carla. I'm starved."

"Enjoy." The auburn-haired waitress with the gorgeous Rubenesque figure actually batted her eyelashes at him. "Anything else I can get you?"

"Thanks, I think we're all set," he said. He turned to his sister, who was smirking at Carla's blatant flirting. "How are Mom and Dad doing?"

CHAPTER 34

"Hey, Dad," Wolfie said, spying his father sitting on the corral fence, watching Gus Casey, their head trainer, working with Tornado, the wildest of the rescued mustangs.

"Hi, son. Come sit and observe a true master. What Gus has done with this horse and some of the others is remarkable."

"Hey, brother," Weezie called as she led a chestnut Morgan out of the barn. "Want to go for a ride? I can saddle Crackers and you can ride Sheba."

"Thanks, sis, but I'm here to talk to Dad. You go ahead."

Weezie studied her brother, then looked from him to her father. Finally, she shrugged. "Okay, I know when I'm a third wheel. Have fun with your guy talk, and I'll see you in an hour or so." She mounted Sheba in one fluid motion and gave her flank a gentle nudge. She soon disappeared over the rise leading to the Loop Trail that ringed the peninsula.

"She's gotten to be an expert, hasn't she?" Wolfie said.

"All those expensive riding lessons are finally paying off."

"No, I mean since you moved down here. She's amazing."

"Yes, she is. I've talked to Gus, and he agrees. I've decided to put her in charge of the riding program—private and group lessons and pony camps. She'll need at least one, maybe two assistants, but she can hire them. Our Weezie's growing up."

"Speaking of growing up… Dad, I'd like to accept the vineyard job, if you still think I'm the man for it."

Richard clapped his hands. "I know you are! Morgan's Fire will be in good hands with you, Zeke, and his assistant, Cara. I can't remember. Have you met them?"

"Zeke yes, his assistant no. Is she of the same vintage?" Wolfie asked, referring to the vintner who was in his seventies.

Richard laughed. "No, no. She's probably about your age. Smart as a whip and cute too."

"You sure she wouldn't be a better fit to manage things?"

"Absolutely not. It's a Morgan company, and it's gonna be run by a Morgan. Your sister set up all the ad copy before she left. I had her profile you as manager, hoping for the best. I can give you a folder of stuff to look over. Once you approve, we'll send everything to the printer and get the website updated."

"How is our PR person, anyway? Have you heard from the sisters?"

"They're having a ball. They've been hiking in Wales and are headed for northern England and the Lakes District today or tomorrow. I think the plan is to travel in Scotland the next week or two then come back down to the southern coast and Cornwall. Then maybe fly to Ireland."

Wolfie whistled. "Must be nice."

"Just what Gail needed. Poor baby. Pam said she mooned around for the first week, but she's perked up now. They've met lots of great people along the way, including a few handsome Englishmen, apparently."

"I saw Tim in town the other day. He looked like shit," Wolfie said.

"Poor guy. Sounds like he's up against the impossible, but you have to admire him for trying to help an old friend."

"Yup." As they watched, the huge mustang reared up, hooves flying. Gus continued to stay calm, holding the lead loosely, talking softly. "He is incredible, isn't he?"

Richard nodded. "Both are, man and horse. Now let's go have some lunch and talk about your travel. I've got many contacts for you, vineyards all over the place happy to have you visit, including the Dillons out in Saguaro."

"Not really a comparable climate," Wolfie said as they walked toward the house.

"No, but Jaybo Dillon's vintner is one of the best in the business, and he's got lots of contacts on the West Coast."

"I'm happy to go out there. I love the Valley, but I think I'll learn more visiting places on Long Island and in Maine."

Richard clapped him on the shoulder. "Whatever you think. You're the boss."

*****

"Yeah! Wolfie said yes to Dad," Pam said as she scrolled through text messages on her phone. They sat in a pub in Grasmere enjoying their dinner of mussels and local vegetables.

"That's great news," Gail said. "He'll be a terrific manager, even though I think it'd be easier for him if he went back for his MBA."

"He's smart. He can do it, and Rich is there to advise him. Oh my God, these mussels are to die for. What's that unusual flavor, do you think?" Pam asked, sopping up the broth with a heel of crusty bread.

"Tastes like anise," Gail said. "They are amazing, as are these root veggies. Wine's perfect too."

Pam nodded, tapping her glass against hers. "Now, sis, we have decisions to make. Do you want to tour around the Lakes a few more days, or head up to Edinburgh?"

"I vote one more day here. I'd love to drive up to New Sawrey to Hill Top Farm," Gail said, referring to the home of Beatrix Potter, the author and illustrator of some of their most beloved childhood stories.

"I'm with you on that," Pam said. "Aunt Cherie would never forgive us for not seeing where Beatrix lived."

Gail smiled at her sister. "So let's stay one more night here. I love this B and B. The next day, we can get up at dawn and head north."

"It's a plan!" Pam said. "We can let them know when we get back. I'm pretty sure the room's ours all week, if we want it."

"Thanks, Pam," Gail said, reaching across the heavy oak table to pat her sister's hand.

"For?"

"For bringing me along. This trip has been really special and just what I needed."

Pam grinned. "I'm glad. Travel heals."

"It also gives one a new perspective on things."

Her sister eyed her. "Such as?"

"Such as, Tim Miller was a fun, exhilarating diversion, but I'm over him. Period. End of story." *Yeah right, and the Easter Bunny will be hopping through the pub door any minute.*

"I like the perspective part, but don't give up on Tim. You guys were great together. Once he gets his friend squared away, he'll be back. Dad said he was crushed when he heard you were away."

At that moment, two brawny men approached their table.

"Evenin', ladies," the taller one said. "I'm Ewan, and this is Marty. Mind if we join you?"

Gail opened her mouth, intending to say they were just leaving, when her sister said, "Of course! We were just thinking about dessert, weren't we, sis?"

Several hours later, the sisters stumbled into the B and B having left Ewan and Marty at the pub. They leaned on each other, giggling like two schoolgirls. Pam stumbled, grabbing hold of Gail's arm. "I definitely did not need that third brandy!"

"We're going to be really sorry in the morning," Gail said, conscious that her speech was somewhat slurred. Fortunately the B and B proprietors were already in bed so their reeling ascent to their room went unobserved. Gail's last thought as she drifted off to sleep was of Tim and his lips on hers. *How will I ever really get over him, especially when we live in the same town?*

CHAPTER 35

It had been five weeks since Gail and Pam Morgan flew to England and almost five weeks since Izzy Hodge had committed herself to the Longwood Rehabilitation Center. Tim had heard little except weekly progress reports from Frankie, who kept in touch with Izzy's attorney. They'd decided that was the wisest course, especially since Izzy had made it clear she wanted nothing to do with him.

He'd been out on the boat since dawn and had just gotten back to the shop when the door swung open and Richard Morgan appeared. "Hey, Tim. I'm not interrupting, am I?"

"No, sir, come on in."

"Where's the blacksmith today?"

"Out at my folks' place, shoeing horses."

Richard nodded. "I've been wanting to talk to him about our horses."

"He should be around tomorrow or maybe later today. Want me to have him call you?"

"That'd be great. Actually, it's you I mostly came to see."

"Oh?"

"I'd like to commission a number of pieces for the farmhouse and also several for the cottages on the property. We've got people moving in, and there's no furniture."

"I'm flattered you thought of me, sir, but I'm kind of slow and not cheap. You could probably go to some of the big furniture places on the way to Providence and pick up everything you need."

"First of all—no more 'sir.' Second, as I'm sure I've told you, I like to support local artisans and want only the best. There's no hurry. I brought a list of our immediate needs."

Richard handed Tim a paper. A quick glance revealed commissions that would pay his rent for five years. Dressers, tables, beds. If he even accepted the work, he'd have to hire help. To do them all himself would take several years.

"Wow, Richard, this is a lot. Can I think about it and get back to you with a time frame and estimated cost?"

"Absolutely. Take your time. We have some furniture we can haul out of storage to get us started."

Tim smiled. "Okay, then. How *is* everything out at the farm?"

"Great. Gus Casey has worked miracles with the wild horses, and his two assistants are terrific too. Weezie should have a riding program in place by midsummer. She's in charge there."

"And the vineyard?"

"Our vintner arrives next week. We've put him and his assistant up in town until their quarters are ready. You don't do built-in bookshelves, do you?"

"Sometimes, but you're better off to get a local carpenter to do it. I can give you a couple of names." He scribbled names and numbers on a slip of paper and handed it to Richard.

"Okay, then."

Still bowled over by the long list, Tim asked, "What style furniture did you have in mind? Any special kinds of wood?"

"I favor clean lines, Shaker style," Richard said. "No curly cues or elaborate carvings. Love pine, maple, cherry. Don't much care for oak."

Tim smiled. "Got it. Okay, I'll work up an estimate and timeline and we can go from there."

"Thanks, son. The world travelers are having a great time, by the way."

Tim nodded, the unspoken question now in the open. He wanted to ask about Gail, but wasn't sure his queries would be welcome or answered. "That's great. Where are they now?"

"Scotland. They've been hiking for several days."

Tim swallowed hard. "How is she?"

Richard met his eyes, his gaze warm. "Gail's my close-lipped child. Always has been. Pam says her spirits are better. The trip's been good for her. I shouldn't tell you this, but she was pretty broken up when she left."

Tim nodded. "All my fault, of course."

"Not all your fault, son. Takes two to make a relationship work. You never know what the future will bring."

"I'm sure you're right. Thanks for this," Tim said, holding up the list.

"We'll talk soon. Do tell the smithy I'm looking for him."

"Will do."

*****

Coop returned hot and dirty a few hours later. Tim had been on the phone most of the time since Richard had departed, seeing who might be available for part-time work. He'd lined up three woodworkers with whom he had contracted before and was leaning back in his chair when Coop strolled in, canvas bags of tools in both hands.

"Hey, buddy, what's up?" Coop threw down his load and headed for the refrigerator. "Beer?"

"Sure," Tim answered. "How were things at Land's End?"

"Great. Your dad spent the day following me around supervising, and your sainted mom made me an amazing lunch."

"Richard Morgan stopped by looking for you."

"What'd he want?" Coop asked, handing him a beer.

"Wants to get you out to the farm to shoe his horses."

"Not this week," Coop said, flopping down in a dirty, half-broken lawn chair.

"He also gave me a list a mile long of commissioned work. I tried to steer him toward Cardis or Jordans, but he insists he wants locally crafted stuff. I've just lined up four guys to help me."

"That's gonna cost a pretty penny," Coop said, leaning back in the rickety chair.

"You know if you don't watch out, you're gonna fall over on your ass," Tim said.

Coop smiled. "I live dangerously, buddy. Did Morgan have anything to say about his traveling daughters?"

Tim narrowed his eyes. "Only that that were having a great time."

"When do they get back?"

"Didn't say."

Coop rolled his eyes. "And you didn't ask?"

"Nope. None of my business."

"Yeah, keep telling yourself that."

They heard a knock at the barn door, and Frankie Brown stepped in. "Hey, guys." She nodded to Coop before turning to Tim. "Got a minute?"

"Sure. Shoot. You can say anything around Coop that you can to me."

"It's about Izzy."

CHAPTER 36

"This is an incredibly dumb idea," Coop said as he drove north to Greenport and the Longwood Rehabilitative Center.

"Maybe so, but I've got you with me, mother hen. So you can step in if needed."

"And don't think I won't!"

"Look, she asked to see me. I'm going. I'll see her, see that she's okay, and then we're done. Frankie and the attorney have found her a place to live when she gets out next week. A halfway house where they'll check up on her. She'll continue counselling and start her community service."

"What about her scumbag friend Ice?"

Tim shrugged. "Let's hope he's a million miles away or he's been arrested again."

As they pulled into the Longwood Center, Tim turned to him. "Thanks for coming. I can take it from here."

"Want me to wait in the lobby?"

"No, I'm all set. Do you mind hanging here? Or feel free to go grab coffee or food and come back."

"Got my water. I'll be here," Coop said. "Good luck."

The attendant led Tim through the main building, a sleek modern structure, walls painted in soft muted colors, furnished in grays and beiges that blended into their surroundings. Plants were everywhere. They reached a set of French doors that opened onto a terraced garden. The young woman turned to him. "She's by the gazebo. Take as much time as you need. When you're ready to go, please come through the building and let someone know."

"Thanks, will do." Tim opened the door and headed to an ornate structure at the center of the garden. He spied her sitting, gazing off into space. As he neared, she turned and smiled.

"Hey," he said softly, relieved at her appearance. Much healthier, she'd put on a little weight and was not quite as skeletal or fragile. Her cheeks had a bit of color.

She stood as he neared her. "Thanks for coming."

They hugged each other stiffly, then sat on a nearby bench.

"So what do they say about your reentry into the real world?"

"Not for a few weeks at least," she said. "I still can't keep much food down."

"Well, you look much better," he said, smiling.

"Thanks. Tim… I want to… I was so messed up. I'm sorry."

"But you're better now."

She nodded. "Can you forgive me?"

"Nothing to forgive. You stay healthy and on the straight and narrow. That's all I want for you."

"I'm not sure what the straight and narrow is," she said softly. "And I'm not at all sure I can do it."

"Sure you can," he said, patting her hand.

"Only thing I was ever good at was being a cop, and look where that landed me. I'll never get a job doing that again." She gazed straight ahead.

"Don't they help with that here? Thinking about jobs? Retraining?"

"I think so, but I'm not there yet."

"You'll find something, Iz. Something good and healthy, so you can have the life you deserve."

"With you?"

"Excuse me?" His heart sank. *What am I gonna say to her? I can't lie, but I don't want to send her spiraling downward.* Honesty. That's what they'd advised when they called to say that Izzy asked to see him. *Honesty it is.*

"I was hoping we might have another chance when I get out?" she said, gazing at him with her pale blue eyes.

"Iz, I'm sorry, but that's not gonna happen. I care about you, I do. A part of me will always love you, but there's no future for us, baby. I'm really sorry."

Chin up, she nodded. "That's okay. I understand. I figured that's what you'd say, what with your girlfriend and all."

"This has nothing to do with Gail," he said quietly. "You and I were over ten years ago when you disappeared. There's no going back."

"No, I guess not," she replied, her voice wistful.

"You'll find your place, Iz. And when you do, I'll be there cheering you on. Promise. You can call anytime if you need me, okay?"

She nodded. "You know, I'm a little tired. I think I'm going to head in."

"Of course. Can I walk you?" He extended his hand, and she placed her small frail hand in it. Tim curled his fingers around hers, and they walked slowly inside.

As they neared the lobby, she stopped. "This is me. I'm down that hall."

"Okay, then. Take care of yourself, Iz." They hugged, and she hurried off, disappearing at the end of a long hallway.

"How'd it go?" came a voice from behind him. It was the same young woman who had escorted him in, a short redhead with bobbed hair and a round freckled face. She wore a pale green tailored uniform, her name, Shelly Wordell, on her ID tag.

"Fine, thanks."

"She's doing great," Shelly said.

"That's good to hear. She wanted to know if we had a future. When I spoke to your colleague the other day, he told me to be honest. I was. Honest, I mean. I told her we didn't have a future together. Will that set her back, do you think?"

"Maybe for a day, but she's learning resiliency. We can work on that in her therapy sessions."

Tim nodded. "She's worried about what she's going to do, jobwise and all."

"We'll get her there. Our recommendation aligns with that of the attorney who has been working on her behalf. When she's ready, she'll go to a halfway house. It's one of the better ones in the system. They'll help with jobs."

"Is there anything I can do?" he said.

"Probably not, except to let her know she has a friend."

"I did."

She extended her hand, which he shook. "Thanks for coming, Tim."

"No problem." As he turned away and headed for the door, Tim felt an enormous weight lifted from his shoulders. A weight he'd been carrying for over ten years. Izzy was still in the woods, but someone was taking care of her. He could let go.

When he reached Coop's truck, his friend was asleep. Tim opened the door, and Coop started awake. "Hey, buddy. How'd it go?"

Tim shrugged. "It's over. Let's go home."

CHAPTER 37

Exactly six weeks after their departure, Gail and Pam returned, tired but exhilarated, eager to share highlights of their travels. Two days after their return, Amy, Rob, and Lucy moved to the farmhouse. Their rooms had been painted and arranged according to their wishes. A local carpenter had installed beautiful shelving units in both rooms and a window seat in Amy's that looked out over the fields. The house was a happy bustle as boxes, bags, and clothes were brought in and moved upstairs. Some of Lucy's belongings were stored in the barn, but she had managed to give away most of what she couldn't bring. A number of her furniture pieces had gone to various properties on the farm, some to Wolfie's apartment, others to the vintner's cottage and his assistant's loft. Even the Caseys had taken a dresser and some chairs for their home that was near completion, tucked in a wooded glen at the property's west corner.

As Gail stood in the kitchen chatting with Amy, Tim's truck pulled in by the barn. "Shit!" she said, then noticed Amy's puzzled, slightly shocked reaction. "Oh, sorry, I just remembered something I needed to do. Excuse me, will you?"

She hurried out of the room and started for the stairs, intending to hide in her room until he departed. Pam caught her in the front hall. "Oh no, you don't. Time to face the music. Besides, he's here to deliver furniture for the kids' rooms. He's going to be in and out. So there's no place to hide."

Gail waved her hands, pacing. "I can't, I can't. I've spent the last six weeks trying to forget him. I can't. I'm not ready!"

The front door opened, and Tim and her father stepped in, each carrying small bedside tables. "Will you look at these?" their father said. "The craftsmanship is exquisite. Hope the kids are happy with them."

Amy walked into the hall and exclaimed, "Oh, I love that. Is that for my room?"

Richard beamed. "Sure is, honey. We'll take it up, unless you'd like to? We've got a few more pieces in the truck."

Amy grabbed the table. "Of course!" and hustled up the stairs, leaving the sisters and the two men.

"Hey, welcome back, ladies," Tim said, gazing from Pam to Gail, his eyes lingering on her. "How was the trip?"

"Great, super," Pam said. "We have lots of pictures we'd be happy to show you. Right, Gail?"

Gail swallowed hard, then said, "Good to see you. Looks like you have a lot of unloading to do, so I'll let you get on with it." Without another word, she turned and headed back to the kitchen.

His two companions looked at Tim, whose face had fallen. Richard patted him on the shoulder. "Give her time, son. She'll come around."

Yeah, right, Tim thought. "Where am I going with this, sir?"

As they made several trips in and out of the house, Tim looked, but never caught another glimpse of Gail. *It's official, she hates me,* he thought as he carried the last load in, a chest for Rob's room. After depositing it upstairs, he met Richard in the driveway.

The older man waved. "I'll follow you to the vineyard because I've got a few things in my truck. Wolfie and the men can help when we get there."

Tim nodded. As he hopped into the truck, he gazed up at the second floor of the farmhouse and thought he saw a curtain move as someone stepped back from the window. *Had to be her,* he thought. *Maybe there's hope there somewhere.*

*****

Later that morning, Pam and Gail called Lynn Casey and invited her to meet them for lunch at the Café. "Love to!" Lynn had said.

At one, the restaurant was full, but they found a table by the window. Lucy had been there with a client, but they departed shortly after the three women arrived. Lynn smiled at the two sisters. "So glad to have some adult time. I love my three kids and Gus, but I miss my women friends, especially Polly."

"Anytime," Gail said, one eye on the street in case Tim happened by.

Pam nodded. "Yes, let's make it a regular thing. I miss having women friends too. Maybe we should start a junior Darn Yarners like Lucy's mom's group?"

Lynn laughed. "Not sure how I'd fit it in. I'm going to start back to work before long and begin the mom juggling act."

"Where?" Pam asked.

"I'm looking for a teaching job, but for the next few years, I'd rather go part-time, and those kinds of jobs are hard to come by. I was so spoiled in the Valley with the ridiculously high salaries they paid us, but thanks to the generosity of your dad and Gus's salary, we can afford for me to take it slow. For starters, I'm going to take your brother's place working at Merlin's Closet with Lucy and Lolly. Then we'll see what opens up."

"Speaking of Lolly, isn't that her ex and Ava's childhood heartthrob?" Pam asked, gazing up as Sandy Rodriguez stepped into the diner with two men.

Lynn nodded. "You know Sandy from childhood?"

Pam waved at him. "He worked for our family one summer. Ava, our sister, had a huge crush on him. He is gorgeous, isn't he?"

"And doesn't he know it," Lynn said. "I've seen him around town a bunch of times, and he always has a different woman on his arm."

"Maybe they're his sisters?" Pam said.

Gail gave her a look. "Yeah, right, and I'm Marilyn Monroe back from the grave."

"Oh gee, he's coming over!" Pam whispered, smiling as the tall, broad-shouldered club owner approached them. His dark wavy hair brushed the collar of his sky-blue sport shirt, and his piercing dark eyes sparkled with interest.

Bedroom eyes, Gail thought, smiling at him. *Dangerous, sexy bedroom eyes.* "Hi," she said.

"Hey, Lynn," he said, nodding to their companion before turning to the sisters. "Well, well, if it isn't the other Morgan girls all grown up. I've been wondering when I'd run into you. I see Ava around and your baby sister Weezie, and I think I caught a glimpse of Gail at the Club a while back? But it's been what, fifteen years at least since I saw you, Pam."

"Probably. Hi, good to see you."

"You've changed," he said, apprising every inch of her.

"Well, I should hope so. The year you were working in Maine, I was three."

"I've got a kind of lunch meeting, so I've gotta go, but we should get together, have a drink. Catch up on old times?"

He directed these remarks to Pam, who was hanging on his every word. "Sure, great," she sputtered. "I've just moved to the village. Love to catch up."

Hook, line, and sinker, Gail thought watching the lion stroll back to his pride. "Why not just fall at his feet and scream 'take me now'?" she said to her sister.

Pam frowned. "What are you talking about?"

Lynn smiled, watching them. "You did let him know you were interested."

"And you were far from subtle about it!" Gail said.

Pam sniffed. "I was just trying to be friendly."

"Friendly is hi, how are you? Drooling goes way beyond that!" Gail said. "Let's order. I'm starved."

As the waitress disappeared with their orders, Gail said, "Watch it with him, sis. That's all I'm saying."

Pam shrugged. "I'll probably never see him again."

"I bet you will," Lynn said. "And why not? You're a beautiful woman, he's drop-dead gorgeous, and you're both single. Have some fun. Just remember who you're dealing with. He's not exactly Mr. Reliable."

"We were discussing a catch-up drink. I wasn't offering to bear his children," Pam said, crossing her arms over her chest.

"He already has a child with Lolly, your stepmother's partner," Gail said. "But let's change the subject. I'm sick of men, except Gus, of course. How are you guys settling into Horseshoe Crab Cove?"

"Well… It's been an adjustment with the baby and all. The older two are really happy at school, so that helps."

"Where is the baby today?" Pam asked.

"Our neighbor, Ruth Penny, is watching her. Ruth is terrific and so good with the kids. Have you met her?"

"No," Gail said.

"She and her husband live next to our rental," Lynn said. "He works at the fishery and she's at home. She's a painter. Actually, a pretty good one. Local scenes. Says she sells well all summer, then business dies down. She's a peach."

"Your cottage on the farm is almost finished, isn't it?" Pam asked.

"Almost. We're planning to move in next month. Your father is the best. I'm sure you know that. He's been so generous and kind. He's given us as long as we want to decide if we want to exercise our option to buy."

Gail smiled at the dark-haired beauty. *Earth mother*, she thought. "If you wait long enough, Dad'll give you the house."

Lynn laughed.

Pam nodded. "She's right. Dad's loaded. He loves to give to those he loves, and he *loves* you guys."

CHAPTER 38

Three weeks passed, and Tim and Gail had not run into each other. She felt like she lived every day on tenterhooks, afraid to go into town lest she see him and burst into tears. It had taken her a week to recover from their chance meeting at the farmhouse. She threw herself into work as they geared up to promote the winery. She and Rich had been writing endless grant applications for funding to support the mustang program. But no matter how busy she was, her mind always returned to him. She missed him terribly.

In the office one day, Lucy popped her head in. "Hey, Gail, I'm meeting my mom and sister for lunch in town. Want to come?"

She hesitated, then said, "Why not? Just let me grab my purse."

The four women settled into a back booth at the Cove Grille, iced teas in front of them. "Where's Pam today?" Harriet asked.

"She has an interview," Gail said. "At the middle school. They're looking for a part-time counselor."

"Is that her interest, working in a school setting?" Helen Winthrop, Lucy's mom, asked. The sixty-something stained-glass artist was remarkably youthful except for her hands, which appeared to be crippled with arthritis. Her waist-length salt-and-pepper hair hung in one long braid down her back, her blue eyes bright and warm. She wore jeans and a long woven top in the same blue shade as her remarkable eyes.

"I think so," Gail said. "She's only worked a little over a year as a social worker, so I suspect she's still finding herself."

Harriet smiled. "Speaking of finding herself, Kyle and I were having dinner at the Bluewater the other night, and we ran into Pam with Sandy Rodriguez."

"What?" Lucy said, looking from her sister to Gail.

Gail raised her hands. "Hold on, hold on, they were just having a catch-up drink."

Lucy turned to Harriet for confirmation. "Is that what you saw too?"

"I think it was dinner, but don't quote me on that. Is there a problem?"

"Not if she wants to date a snake in the grass, low-life Casanova," Lucy said.

Gail stared at her normally calm, affable stepmother. "That's a little harsh, isn't it?"

Helen nodded, frowning at Lucy. "I've always found him to be a perfect gentleman."

"He's also the son of your dear friend, and he's not trying to date you," Lucy said, gazing across the crowded restaurant. "And speaking of your friend, here comes Rosa now."

Rosa Rodriguez was one of Helen's Darn Yarners. As she approached, her smile broadened when she spotted her dear friend. "Hello, ladies, great to see you! Has Carla taken your order?" Rosa hugged Helen and nodded to the others.

Harriet smiled up at her. "Not yet, but we're not in a hurry."

"I'll be happy to put it in. What would you like?" Rosa pulled a small pad from her apron, jotted down their choices, and chatted for a few minutes before heading for the kitchen.

"Do you really think a son of Rosa's could be all bad?" Helen directed her remarks to her oldest daughter.

"Mother, I know Sandy has a lot of charm, but he also broke my best friend's heart."

Harriet gave Gail a look as she gazed from her mother to her sister. "Well, it didn't appear that he was proposing marriage, so let's not get too worked up.

And FYI—Carla's one of Sandy's former girlfriends, or maybe still a girlfiend, so a change of topic might be wise?"

Suddenly, Lucy laughed. "You're right, of course. Listen to me! What do I know? Please forgive the petulant outburst."

Gail smiled at her stepmother. *She's probably right on the money, but everyone has to make their own mistakes in love and life.* She then turned to Helen. "So what's new with you, Helen? Pam loves living next to your buddy Frankie, by the way."

"I'm glad. It's good for Frankie too. That house has had a succession of tenants, some considerate, some not."

"What's Frankie been up to lately?" Harriet asked. "She's always got some new iron in the fire."

With a glance toward Gail, Helen said, "She's had a few stained-glass commissions, two of which we worked on together. Frankie's much better at soldering than I am."

"What about her investigating?" Harriet said. "Frankie's a PI. Did you know that, Gail?"

Gail saw Helen hesitate, probably out of consideration for her feelings, so she said, "She's been helping Tim to support his friend Izzy Hodge, right?"

Helen nodded. "I believe her work there is done. The young woman was released to a halfway house last week."

Gail's jaw dropped. "Oh?" Then, because she couldn't stop herself, she asked, "So Tim must be with her, supporting her?"

Helen shook her head. "I don't know all the particulars, but I know Frankie said he made things very clear to the girl that they had no future. Tragic case, really. She was a real cute teenager. Smart too."

Lucy glanced at her mother before turning to Gail. "She was a year ahead of Harriet and Tim's sister Karen in school."

"So I understand," Gail said, suddenly wishing she was a million miles away. *"He made things very clear to the girl that they had no future." He broke things off with his soul mate!*

"I hope they know what they're doing releasing her and that she'll get the support she needs from here on out," Harriet said. "Mom's right. Izzy is smart, and she was a great person."

They continued chatting about life over lunch. Mostly, the sisters talked and Helen and Gail listened. Gail was so distracted with thoughts about Tim that she started when she realized Helen had asked her a question. "I'm sorry, I was daydreaming," she said, sitting up straighter in her chair.

Helen smiled. "No worries. I just asked how you enjoyed your travels."

"We had a wonderful trip," Gail said, and they spent the rest of lunch chatting about her adventures in the UK.

CHAPTER 39

"When did she come by?" Tim asked, staring at Coop.

"Like I said. About an hour ago."

"Why didn't she just call?"

Coop shrugged. "Said she wanted to find you in person."

Tim frowned. "Did she say where she was going?"

"Nope."

Tim rang Frankie's cell. This time, she answered, her voice grave. "Hey, Tim. I'm in Northport, at Fred's Diner on Route 2. Can you meet me up here?"

"What's happened?" he said.

"I'd rather talk in person. See you soon?"

"I'm on my way," Tim said.

"What's up?" Coop asked as his friend slipped his cell phone into his pocket.

"She wouldn't tell me, so it must be bad news."

"I'm coming," Coop said. "In fact, I'm driving. Let's go."

*****

Fred's Diner was a local landmark, one of the last silver-sided behemoths in the area. Frankie was sitting in a booth by the door when Coop and Tim drove up. She came outside to greet them, her face betraying the gravity of the situation.

Tim flew out of the truck and ran to meet her. "What is it?"

"I'm sorry to have to tell you this, but the police have found a body. A woman's body."

"It couldn't be her. She's at the halfway house, isn't she?"

"Apparently, she walked out three days ago and disappeared. They've been looking for her, but she simply vanished."

"Where?"

"The body's at the county morgue," Frankie said, looking from one man to the other.

"I mean, where did they find her?" Tim said.

"In a motel in Northport near the docks."

"Jesus Christ! It can't be her. It just can't," Tim said, tears rimming his eyes. "After all her hard work. She looked great when I saw her."

Coop put his hand on his friend's shoulder. "So what do we do from here?"

Frankie looked at Tim. "They need someone to identify the body. There are no next of kin that they can find."

Tim nodded. "Let's go, then."

They followed Frankie's car and parked on a side street, walking the two blocks to the Northport Police Department. The two-story granite building housed several small courtrooms and, in its basement, the county morgue. As they headed for the front doors, Coop said, "Why don't you let me go, buddy? I can identify her, and you can remember her as she was when you saw her at Longwood."

Tim shook his head. "I've gotta do it. I owe it to her."

The three made their way in through metal detectors and were escorted downstairs to the morgue. A technician behind the desk let them in. "Aaron Whiting. I'm the only one here," he said. "I can take you back to see her, then let the officers know."

The four walked back until they stood next to a closed door. "You ready?" Aaron opened the door to a spare room with single table, body on it, draped in white. When they stood beside it, Aaron looked at Tim. He nodded, and the technician lifted the sheet. It was Izzy, her face deathly pale, her neck with an angry purple band around it.

Aaron looked from one to the other of them. "She was strangled, but there was also enough fentanyl in her system to kill off a city block."

"Poor baby," Frankie whispered.

"I'm sorry, but I need a positive ID," Aaron said.

"It's her," Tim said, his voice hoarse, tears in his eyes. "It's Isabel Hodge. Have they caught the bastards who did this to her?"

"You'd have to speak to the cops," Aaron said. "If it's any consolation, she may have been close to death with the fentanyl and not have felt the pain of the strangulation. It's odd they even bothered. Whoever gave her the drugs had to know they'd kill her."

"What a waste!" Tim said, pounding the table with his fist.

Coop placed a hand on his shoulder. "Come on, let's get out of here."

"No, I'm not leaving her here in this shithole."

Frankie came around the table and placed her hands on his upper arms, her grip strong. "Izzy is not here anymore, Tim. She's at peace, and we need to leave her. Aaron will take good care of her, won't you?"

"No worries, man. When they say we can release her, do you know where she's going?"

"I'll arrange with a funeral home. She wanted to be cremated," Tim said.

Coop stared at him, his eyes registering surprise.

"We talked about it when we first dated," Tim said. "She was adamant. Wanted to be cremated and her ashes taken out into the middle of the river to be scattered."

Aaron nodded. "If you give me a number, I'll let you know when the funeral home can collect her."

"Come on, then," Frankie said, pulling Tim's arm, Coop on his other side. At the door, Tim turned and took one last look at the tiny body, fully covered again, then allowed himself to be escorted out.

Once upstairs, Frankie said, "We can talk to the officers who found her, if they're here, but I doubt they'll tell you much."

"Come on, then," Tim said. "Let's ask for them."

Only one of the men who found her was on duty and in the station: Angus Farley. He appeared and ushered them back to an empty room. "Sorry, I don't have an office. This is the best I can do. How can I help you folks?"

Tim sat hard on one of the five chairs in the room, arms on the cold metal table. "Have you gotten anywhere finding the bastards who murdered her?"

"We have some leads. My partner and two other guys are checking one out as we speak. I stayed back because Ms. Brown here told me you'd be coming in. Have you guys got any idea who might want to harm her?"

Tim shrugged. "Until recently, I hadn't seen or heard from her for ten years. I haven't got a fucking clue. She wouldn't tell me shit about the lowlifes she hung with."

Coop leaned forward. "There was a guy, Ice, who she committed the robbery with. He was supposedly her friend, but he was a real scumbag. If he didn't do it, he might know who did."

Officer Farley looked at him. "Short, scraggly, dark tattoos all over his face and arms?"

Coop nodded. "That's a pretty good description of Ice."

"He was in the room with her. In addition to a beating, some of his fingers were missing. He also had speedball of fentanyl that killed him long before they could've strangled him."

"Jesus," Coop said. "Who the hell are these guys?"

"We think they're part of a gang tied to the cartels. They usually don't operate in this area, but they brought a large shipment of drugs in by boat, and somehow, this Ice character was involved in a very low-level capacity. He was clearly expendable once they got the drugs in. I suspect your friend was just in the wrong place at the wrong time, so she had to go too. These guys are probably long gone, but we're doing our best."

"Ice didn't seem like that big of a player," Coop said, shaking his head. "He reminded me of the wannabe biker gangs we had around here in high school."

Farley nodded. "That's as accurate a description as any. He was an addict who gambled big whenever he had cash. My guess is he caught their eye somewhere, maybe Foxwoods, and they recruited him with promises of money and drugs. Or maybe he owed someone big money so this was his payback. Either way, he's dead and can't tell us anything."

Frankie stood up. "Thank you, Officer Farley. We'll get out of your hair now. If you do manage to catch the perpetrators, please let us know, if you can."

Tim and Coop followed her out, mute and shaken. On the thirty-minute drive back to Horseshoe Crab Cove not a word was exchanged between them. When Coop parked in the lot by their workshop, he said, "Want company tonight, buddy?"

"Thanks, Coop. I'll be fine."

"Well, call if you change your mind."

Tim waved over his shoulder as he headed for his own truck. *Yeah, right, I'll be fine. Izzy's in the morgue, and the woman I love hates my guts. How much finer can I get?*

CHAPTER 40

The family had just finished dinner and Gail and Pam were washing dishes when their stepmother came into the room. "That was delicious, Callie," Lucy said, following the housekeeper to the pantry, where she was putting dishes and cutlery away.

"Thanks. Spring lasagna's one of my favorite recipes," Callie replied.

Lucy came back into the room and stood next to Gail. "I'm afraid I have some bad news. I'm not sure you even want to know, but I'm going to relay it anyway."

Gail set down her dishcloth and turned to Lucy, Pam following suit. "What is it?" Gail asked.

"My mom just called. Frankie was at her house for supper and just left. Earlier today, Frankie met Tim in Northport because they found the body of Izzy Hodge, and someone had to identify it."

Gail clapped her hand over her mouth, staring at Lucy, eyes wide. "She's dead? I thought she was in rehab."

"Got out recently and was living at a halfway house. She disappeared from there several days ago and wound up murdered in a sleazy motel in Northport."

"How?" Pam asked.

"She was strangled and also had a lethal amount of fentanyl in her system. Her friend with whom she was committing the robberies was found with her."

"Ice?" Gail said.

"Yes. He's dead too, apparently."

"How horrible," Pam said, hugging her sister's shoulders.

Lucy nodded. "Yes, very sad. Izzy was a sweet girl when we knew her in high school. Such a tragedy that life took her to such dark places."

Gail untied her apron and threw it on the counter. "I've got to go."

"Wait!" Pam said. "You don't even know where he is."

Lucy exchanged looks with Pam. "Coop drove him back here, but Frankie didn't know what they did. Maybe he went out to his folks' place."

"I'd still like to check in. Just in case." Gail grabbed her bag in the front hall and hurried to her car, ignoring the pleas of her sister and Lucy to wait.

*****

Tim sat in the apartment, the light fading as twilight descended. He hadn't bothered to turn on a light and preferred sitting with a beer in the semidarkness. He thought back to his visit to Longwood and wondered if his words had driven Izzy to this. *Did she go back to her hideous life because I took all hope away from her?*

A knock at the door startled him. Assuming it was either Coop or a member of his family, he considered not answering. *They'll go away eventually.* The knocks were tentative—*couldn't be Coop*—and something told him his family would be calling his name, *loudly*. Finally, he rose and went to the door. He opened the door and found Gail standing there.

Without a word, she stepped forward and folded her arms around him. "I'm so sorry."

For several minutes, he held on to her for dear life, her warmth and presence comforting to his frayed emotions. It had been nearly two months since he'd touched her, and he was overcome with gratitude. Eventually, the cool evening breeze called him back, and he released her. "Come in?"

She followed him into the dark apartment, waiting for him to turn on a light. When he didn't, she went to a switch by the door, and soft light flooded the room. "Is that okay?" she asked.

Tim nodded.

"Have you had anything to eat?" she said.

He shook his head.

She gazed around, spying four empty beer bottles on the table beside his recliner. "Shall I make something or grab some takeout?"

He shrugged, saying nothing as he sat back in the recliner.

"Why don't I check the fridge?" she said, crossing the room. She found eggs, vegetables, cheese, and bread and took them out. In no time, she assembled ingredients for an omelet and served it with buttered toast.

"Thanks," he said, giving her a crooked smile. "You're not eating?"

"Already had supper at home." She sat in a straight-backed chair beside him, relieved to see him take the plate and begin eating.

He set the fork down. "How did you find out?"

"Lucy's mom called. She and Frankie had dinner together."

"Small town," he said, taking another mouthful of eggs. "This is good, by the way. Thank you."

"Is there anything else I can do for you?" she asked.

"No, this is great."

"Tim, I don't want to intrude if you'd rather be alone. I just wanted to be sure you were all right."

He smiled. "Whatever that means. Right now, I'm feeling like a bastard, wondering if I drove her to it."

Gail stared at him. "How is that possible?"

"I went to see her at Longwood. The rehab place. She wanted to get back together when she got out. I told her that wasn't gonna happen. I thought being honest and upfront was important, but now I'm not so sure."

"You don't blame yourself for her death?"

"If I'd been there the day she checked out of Longwood, taken her to the halfway house, let her know I was still there? Maybe that would have given her hope, kept her strong. Instead, what did she do? Ran back to the only friend she had, that sleazeball, lowlife Ice. They were found dead together."

"Oh, Tim, I'm so sorry."

"Me too. I've pretty much messed up my entire life the past two months. I lost you, then this." He set down the empty plate. "Gail, I meant what I said to Izzy. There was nothing left for her and me. Ever."

"But?" There was so much she wanted to ask him, but didn't know where to begin.

Suddenly, they heard voices on the stairs, several of them calling his name. "Here comes the Miller cavalry," he said, giving her an apologetic look. "My mind's mush tonight anyway, but I'd love to talk soon."

Gail stood and pressed his hand. "Of course. I'll wash up the supper things and let your family visit." Plate in hand, she went to the door, opening it to find Karen and her parents.

"Gail, oh, hello," Faith Miller said. "Are we interrupting?"

"No, please come in. I was just leaving." Gail hurriedly washed up as the three Millers offered condolences and conversed in hushed tones. Afterward, she grabbed her purse, caught Tim's eye, and waved as she went to the door. He mouthed *thank you*, then turned back to his family.

With rioting emotions, Gail drove home. *He told Izzy they had no future.* "I lost you," *he said. Is that true? Has he lost me, or is this just the beginning?*

Pam and Lucy were waiting in the family room when she returned. "Where's Dad?" Gail asked. "I should think he'd want to be in on this."

"Down at the barn with Weezie. One of the horses is unwell. They're waiting for Kyle to come and check him out," Lucy said.

Pam gazed at Gail, concern in her eyes. "You okay?"

Gail flopped down on the sofa. "Yes. What a nightmare for Tim."

"How's he holding up?" Lucy asked.

"Okay. His parents and Karen came, so I left. Think I'll head up to bed." Not waiting for them to say more, she headed for the stairs, bone weary but calmer than she'd been on the ride home. *I'll think about things tomorrow when my head clears. If it ever does!*

CHAPTER 41

Lucy had an early meeting at the office and Pam a job interview, so it was just Richard and Gail at breakfast. "So I heard you saw your guy last night, honey?"

"He's not my guy, but yes, I saw him briefly." She forced a smile. She loved her father, but wasn't ready to talk about Tim right now.

"Tragic about his friend. What a short, sad life."

"Yes," Gail said, setting down her fork. Callie's johnnycakes were delicious, but she had suddenly lost her appetite.

Richard regarded her with kind eyes. He could always read her like a book. "I'm sorry, baby. I shouldn't pry. Forgive me?"

Gail smiled at him. "Always. How's Crackers?" she asked, referring to the ill horse from the previous evening.

"She'll be fine. Kyle diagnosed colic and pumped her full of fluids. He also recommended changes in her diet. More foraging and field grass, less grains."

"He's a good vet, isn't he?"

"The best. What's your plan today?"

"I have some errands in town, then I'm going out to the vineyard to take some photos for the brochure. We may want to hire a professional when we're further along, but I'm pretty sure I can get a few good ones that'll work for now."

"Good to have you back on the job, honey. Wasn't the same without you."

"Thanks, Dad. It's good to be back."

"Maybe later today, you'd like to take a ride with your old man? I've been riding a bit and want to keep in practice."

"Is Crackers up to it? I'm sure I'm not ready to ride one of the mustangs, thank you just the same."

"Kyle said she's fine to go out. Do her good."

Gail rose and kissed her father's cheek. "Okay, Dad, I'll see how the day goes, but if you find another taker, ride out with them. See you."

*****

Gail drove into the village and parked on the street. She needed to go to the stationery store and Averill's, but soon found herself at the end of the street. She strolled across the parking lot next to Tim and Coop's workshop and knocked on the door. When she entered, she found Coop hammering out what looked like some kind of decorative shovel. He nodded as she passed, motioning with his head to the other workshop. She found Tim sanding the drawers of a beautiful cherry dresser.

"Morning!" she called.

Startled, he straightened up, set the sander aside, and brushed dust from his front. "Hey."

"I'm doing errands in town and thought I'd check in and see how you're doing."

"Okay, thanks." He indicated a bench, and they sat side by side.

"Anything I can do to help?"

"No. Thanks, though. They're releasing her body today. She'll be cremated. There'll be a small service this weekend."

"I'd like to come as your friend, if that would be okay?" she asked, meeting his eyes.

"Of course, if you want, but don't feel you have to."

She reached over and took his hand. "I want to."

Tim sat up and looked away before meeting her eyes again. "Listen, Gail, I know you mean well and I'm grateful. Really, I am. I care about you and your well-being, but I'm pretty messed up right now. I don't know a lot of things, but one thing I do know is that you deserve to be with someone much saner and more stable than me."

"You've just had a shock, that's all."

"Maybe a shock of reality? I don't want to drag you down with me. Does that make sense?"

Fighting back tears, she said, "Yes... No... I don't know. So what do you want of me?"

"I want you to go your own way and forget about me."

"That's pretty difficult. We live in the same town, and we're bound to run into each other."

"Friends, then?" he asked, extending his hand.

Gail nodded, taking his hand, biting her lip to keep from crying.

"Listen, I've got work to do, and you probably have much better things to do than hang out with me, right?"

Gail stood abruptly. "Of course. I'll let you get back to work."

Without another word, she turned and strode out. By the time she passed Coop, tears were streaming down her cheeks, but she kept going, hurrying out into the sunlight.

Coop set down his tools and crossed to the other workroom. "What the hell did you do, you big jerk?"

Tim put up his hands. "Not now, Coop!"

"That woman, who loves you, by the way, just ran out of here in tears. If you let the best thing that's ever happened to you get away, you're a bigger asshole than I thought."

Tim's eyes flashed fire. "It's for the best."

"Yeah right," Coop said. "Elise Nolan's office is four doors down. She's a terrific therapist. Do us all a favor and make an appointment before you screw up your life even more."

Coop slammed the workshop door on his way out, leaving Tim staring at the door feeling numb and stupid. *A hundred sessions with Elise Nolan can't fix what's wrong with me,* he thought, then returned to his sanding.

CHAPTER 42

On a drizzly Saturday afternoon, villagers filed into the small Quaker Meeting House at the north end of town. Tim had chosen this venue because Izzy, while not religious, had loved the quiet and simplicity of the Quaker service. The aunt who raised her had attended Meeting for Worship every Sunday, and sometimes her niece accompanied her. In high school, Tim had often tagged along and still went to the occasional meeting. After each, he told himself he should attend more regularly. Sitting in silence surrounded by one's community had been comforting to him, especially in the years after Izzy's disappearance.

Gail came to the service with her family, Ava, Dan, Pam, Weezie, Richard, and Lucy. At Frankie's urging, all the Darn Yarners came to support Faith Miller's son. Most of the Miller family were there, as were several teachers who remembered the bright, passionate woman who had been so proud to graduate at the top of her police academy class. The congregation also included a smattering of locals, including Coop, his parents, and younger sister Bridget. When all were assembled, Kitty Hale, clerk of the Meeting, stood with ramrod-straight posture to explain the meeting procedures. After reading a short poem, she welcomed people who might feel the urge to speak. No one did. Silence prevailed for the entire forty-five minutes. Finally, Kitty rose, shaking hands with the people to either side of her, signaling that the meeting had concluded.

As people filed out, Gail caught a glimpse of Tim heading for his truck, Coop at his side. She wanted to go to him, to hug him, to offer words of comfort, but she suspected that such gestures would not be welcome. Arm linked with Lucy's, Frankie appeared at her side. "He's off to spread her ashes."

Gail looked at her. "Alone?"

"I think Coop's going with him," Frankie said. "Best to let them get on with it."

As if I have a choice, Gail thought, following her family to the cars.

*****

Tim steered the boat out into the channel, his friend sitting at the bow. The river was calm. When they reached the middle of the river, Tim cut the engine, and they drifted in the quiet of late afternoon. The two friends had barely spoken since they left the Meeting House. Now Coop gazed at his friend, unable to read his mood. Finally, he said, "Did she say where?"

"Excuse me?"

"Where she wanted to be sprinkled?"

Tim glanced down at the copper urn on the deck, then met Coop's eyes. "Hell, I don't know. We were kids. It was one vague, half-baked conversation. I just wanted to make a decision and be done with all this."

Coop grinned. "And here I was thinking you had it all planned out."

"Yeah, right."

"This looks like a nice calm spot."

"I guess." Tim picked up the urn and unscrewed the lid. A slight breeze blew off the stern. When he upended the urn, the ashes scattered behind them, drifting with the tide. He whispered, "Bye, sweet girl." When the container was empty, he fingered it for a minute, raised it to his lips, then chucked it and the lid over too.

Coop watched them sink out of sight, then turned to him. "Is that what you do?"

Tim shrugged. "Hell if I know. Got a beer?"

Coop grabbed two from the small cooler, popped the lids, and handed one to him. "To Izzy. May she rest in peace."

Tim nodded. "Yup, a peace she sure didn't have in life."

They drifted for a while, drinking several beers in quick succession. Finally, Tim said, "Guess we'd better get back before my folks send out the Coast Guard. Thanks, Coop. You're a good friend."

Coop smiled. "Damn straight. You know who else is a good friend? Gail Morgan."

"Don't start."

"Did you even speak to her at the service?"

"Nothing to say."

"I know this has been a rough day, but I gotta say this, buddy. You're an ass."

"I couldn't agree more."

"Geez, you are in a mood. Where's the 'fuck you Coop, I'm deep-sixing you if you don't shut up'?"

Tim smiled. "Not a bad idea. I made an appointment with the Nolan woman Monday. Happy?"

"Relieved."

"Never mind that she was in diapers when we were in high school," Tim said, starting the engine.

"Just means she's young and has an agile mind."

"And no life experience."

"Overrated. Life experience sure hasn't helped you. Me either. Most guys our age are settled down with families."

"Or getting divorces."

"I want kids. Don't you?" Coop asked.

"Maybe someday."

"That someday better come soon unless we want to be two old men walkin' into kindergarten."

Tim opened the throttle, and they headed toward the docks. *Do I want a family? Kids? Not unless I'm with someone like Gail…and I've pretty much ensured that's not happening.*

CHAPTER 43

"Come in," Elise Nolan said, standing aside to let Tim pass into her inner office. She had been waiting for him, the door between consulting room and waiting area ajar. "Would you like tea or water?"

"I'm good, thanks," he said, watching as the limber therapist curled herself into one of two overstuffed chairs, waving him into the other. Her brown hair was cut in a short pixie style that suited her. She wore loose gray sweats as if she intended to go for a run after their session.

Her coal-black eyes were warm as they met his. "How can I help?"

"Honestly, I'm not convinced you can, but people I respect and care about recommended you."

"Why would they do that, do you think?"

"'Cause I'm a mess. Can I give you a short summary?"

Elise nodded. "Of course, please."

Tim told her about Izzy, about their history together, and recent events. He also told her about Gail, their whirlwind affair and recent estrangement. He spoke for what seemed like hours, and Elise listened. Occasionally, she nodded or asked for clarification, but by and large, she remained silent. Finally, he said, "So here I am, grieving again for the loss of someone I once loved very much and feeling guilty about her death. I've also driven away someone for whom I care deeply."

Elise nodded, then said, "Of all those issues you just related, is there one around which you would most like to get clarity and perhaps peace?"

"Gail."

"How so?"

"I drove her away. Now, selfishly, I miss her, but I feel like I don't deserve her."

Elise's eyes widened slightly. "Why is that?"

Despite roiling emotions, Tim gave her a crooked smile. "I could say it's the class difference. Her father's a billionaire, and my parents are farmers."

The therapist raised her eyebrow. "Is that really what you think?"

"Hell no. I hurt her. Grievously. That's why I don't deserve her. After our brief but incredibly intense relationship, I go and tell her another woman is part of my soul."

"What about Gail?"

"Excuse me?"

"Is she a part of your soul?"

"The deepest part. No shallow end there," Tim said.

"A nautical metaphor—how lovely," she said, smiling. "So is there a way to undo this hurt?"

"Gail's the most grounded, compassionate person I know. She wouldn't hurt a fly. She has an innocence and naiveté that I trampled all over. Then she was there when Izzy and her scumbag friend tried to assault my best friend with a knife."

"Did Gail experience ill effects or blame you for that?"

He shook his head. "She was incredibly strong and understanding. I mean, the incident freaked her out, but she was still there for me."

"So why did you push her away?"

"I thought, and still think, it's for her own good."

Elise uncurled her legs and sat up. "Doesn't Gail get to decide that?"

"Of course, but she's kind and caring. She wouldn't leave someone she cares about in the lurch. Ever."

"Yet that's what you've done to her. Wouldn't you say 'left her in the lurch' is a fairly accurate description of your actions?"

Tim ran his fingers through his thick curls. "Hell, when you put it that way, I suppose I did. I just wanted her as far away from the nightmare with Izzy as possible."

"Now that's over."

"Thanks to me!"

Elise looked over at him with a stern gaze. "That's something we should definitely explore. Your guilt about Izzy's death. We're out of time, but my next client cancelled just before you arrived. Would you like to chat a little about that?"

"Pretty simple. When I went to see her at Longwood, she was looking for hope, and I killed it."

"By telling her you couldn't be together?"

He nodded. "Maybe if I'd just played along till she was healthier, she'd have been stronger."

"So you saw no future for the two of you?"

"Nope."

"Can you explain that a little?"

"I was crazy in love with Izzy during high school, but some of that faded during our college years, long before she went to the academy. She became like a sister more than a girlfriend, and I'm pretty certain the sober, sane Izzy felt the same about me. We actually talked about it just before she went to the academy. I mean, we were still together and trying to figure out whether the way we were feeling was just normal for couples who'd been together a long time.

"The academy changed her, and she got pretty tight with some of her colleagues. Then the undercover work started, and the drugs. At that point, I was trying to hang on to get her clean, but my feelings had definitely changed, hers too. Finally, she left, and I fell apart. It's taken years to pick up the pieces, and I guess the last few weeks prove I still have work to do there."

Elise touched her finger to her lip and said, "Hmm… A woman you once loved comes back after ten years and steals from you and your dear friend. That would be pretty unsettling to most people. She and her accomplice also accosted someone, two someones, you care about. Again, very unsettling."

"Do you have much experience with addicts?" he asked, eyes meeting hers.

"A bit."

"Do you think I'm right? About the difference hope might have made to her that day at Longwood?"

"Honestly? No. She was clean at that moment, but still very much an addict. Coping with one's addiction is a lifelong process with many years of hard work. It's something you deal with every day, every hour, every minute. She hadn't even started. First steps would have been for her to make healthy connections on the outside. That's the mission of halfway houses. To help addicts integrate. I don't know where she was, but I'm assuming there were caring people committed to helping her."

He nodded. "Frankie checked it out for me. She was really impressed."

"So it was Izzy's choice to turn her back on that help. That choice is about her, not you. If she cared about you, she'd be happy that you found Gail, but addiction often robs one of empathy and caring. It doesn't sound like you'd even entered into the equation for the past ten years. Why would that be different now? Your honesty was exactly what she needed."

"Maybe," he said, gazing downward.

"Do you love Gail?"

Tim looked up, surprised at the question. "Yes," he said.

"That seems like a good place to stop today," Elise said. "If you'd like to meet again, I'll ask you to think about what you just said for homework. You love Gail. Where do you go from here?"

As Tim walked down Main Street to the workshop, he thought about the past ninety minutes. *I do love Gail, more than life itself. So what the hell am I going to do about it?*

CHAPTER 44

Wednesday morning Gail, Weezie, Pam, and Rich sat at the dining room table with their father and Wolfie.

Gail gazed around at her siblings and said, "This is the first one of these since before the honeymoon."

Richard nodded. "And our first with Pam and Wolfie. I invited Pammie even though she's not joining the firm just yet."

"Never," Pam said, smiling at him.

"Never say never," her father said, winking at her. "I'm thrilled to have our winery manager with us. That's something we should decide. What should Wolfie's title be?"

"I think the accepted term is vineyard manager," Rich said. "That doesn't mean we have to stick to that. When Wolfie's traveling around, he can see what other vineyards do."

"It would be great to decide sooner rather than later for the website," Gail said. "It's due to go live in a couple of weeks. We've been working on profiles of Zeke and his assistant, as well as one of Wolfie."

"Good luck with that," Wolfie said. "I've been checking out other websites and managers or directors have long résumés in the business. I hope my nonexistent one doesn't scare people off."

"No chance of that," Richard said. "Besides, people expect unconventional from Morgan companies."

"And I'm guessing no one looks as cool as you brother," Weezie said, giving him a high five.

Gail had woken up achy and tired. As the conversation went on, she found it more and more difficult to follow. In the back of her mind, Tim was always there as a sad distraction, but this was something else. As she reached out and took a sip from her water, the room began to spin.

Rich, who was across the table, gave her a funny look. "Hey, sis, you okay?"

Gail shook her head. "I'm actually not feeling very well. If it's okay, I'm going to lie down for a bit."

"Of course, baby," her father said. "You go right ahead."

She pushed back the chair and attempted to stand, but her legs wouldn't cooperate. They felt like wet noodles. Finally, using the table for support, she managed to stand, but the room now spun out of control and she felt nauseous. When she tried to take a step, she began to fall. Wolfie grabbed hold of her before she could crash to the floor. "Okay, okay, got ya," he said, gazing around the table as he lifted her in his strong arms. "What do you think?" he asked, as Gail's eyes fluttered shut and she fainted. "She feels really warm, like she has a fever."

"I think she needs to be seen by a doctor. Now!" Richard said.

"I'll get the car," Pam said.

Rich put up his hand. "No, I'm calling an ambulance."

*****

"Somebody's in trouble," Coop said as he helped Tim carry a commission to his truck.

A coldness gripped Tim's chest as they listened to the ambulance's siren fade away. "Hope it's no one we know."

"Who would that be? We know everyone in this one-horse town. This is a really cool piece, by the way. One of your best."

"Thanks, it was the client's idea," Tim said, carefully placing one end of the maple coffee table into the truck bed. The rectangular top was simple except for a beautiful inlay at its center showing a long-legged blue heron standing in a marsh. The subtle colors and delicate workmanship exquisite, it was truly a work of art and one of a kind.

Once the coffee table was stowed, Tim wrapped it in an old quilt and roped it securely to the side of the truck. "Want me to bring lunch on my way back? I'm going right by Buster's," he said, referring to a local burger place between the village and Leeside, where Tim's clients lived.

"Double mushroom bacon Swiss burger and curly fries," Coop said without a second's hesitation.

"You got it. Anything to drink?"

"Thanks, I'm good with water. I thought you were seeing the shrink today?"

"She's not a shrink, and I saw her yesterday."

"Helping?"

"A bit. I haven't resorted to self-flagellation in the past few days, so that's progress."

"Good. What's she say about Gail?"

"None of your damn business," Tim said, heading for the cab of his truck.

"If she isn't telling you to grab hold of that woman before it's too late, then you'd better get a new shrink."

Tim rolled his eyes, not bothering to correct Coop's misnomer. "That's not the way therapy works. I have to get there, figure things out for myself."

"Geez, I'll be an old man by then, buddy."

Tim started the truck. "See you in a couple of hours tops."

On the drive to Leeside, Tim thought about the past few weeks and his three conversations with Elise Nolan. She and everyone else was right, of course. He was not at fault for Izzy's death. Frankie had visited the halfway house and spoken to the director. She and her assistant told her that Izzy's short stay had been unremarkable. She had kept to herself and was eager to start her mandated probation job at a nearby laundromat. Frankie told Tim that they saw a frail but strong young woman ready to turn her life around.

So what had happened? Clearly, her friend Ice had gotten in touch with her. Izzy had no phone but was allowed to take walks every day around the neighborhood. Somehow, he'd found her and lured her away. Tim had wanted to hire Frankie to continue to look into the case, but his mother had begged him not to. Faith had spoken to him right after the funeral, saying, "It's too dangerous, honey. I love Frankie. Izzy's gone, so please let it go. I don't want to lose my friend too." And he had acquiesced.

Would it have mattered if I'd been waiting on the outside with open arms? She still had to live in the halfway house for eight months. Ice found her in three days. It's him she's been with for the past ten years, not me.

He and Elise had also talked about Gail and his feelings for her. He did love Gail, he was sure of that, but also felt responsible for her well-being. *Yes, it might take Gail a little to get over me, but it is for the best.* When he'd said those words to Elise, she'd almost laughed him out of the office. Then she'd said, "Best for whom?" in a stern voice.

Ernie and Betsy Plante, his clients in Leeside, greeted him with open arms, oohing and aahing at their beautiful coffee table. Ernie helped him carry it in, Betsy at his side urging him to be careful. When it was in place in their living room, Betsy said, "How 'bout something cool to drink before you head back? Iced tea? Water? Lemonade?"

"I'd love a lemonade," Tim said.

Betsy waved her hands. "You and Ernie head out to the patio. I'll be right with you."

The Plantes lived in a rambling one-story home, with gardens and mature trees shading the two-acre property. Bald, short, and round, Ernie was wearing the same outfit he always wore—khakis, a blue shirt, and boat shoes. Betsy was in lime-green capris, flowered jersey, and green leather flip-flops, her short blonde hair perfectly coifed. The men had barely taken seats when she appeared with a tray of lemonades in tall frosted glasses and a plate of brownies.

"Here, honey, help yourself," she said, sitting beside her husband on a wicker settee.

Tim took a long drink of lemonade and sighed. "You've got a beautiful place here."

"We like it," Ernie said, patting his wife's knee.

"Did you put in all the gardens?" Tim asked.

Betsy nodded. "Sure did. I'm a forty-six-year veteran of the Leeside Garden Club. The whole gang helps from time to time. Now it's mostly maintenance, and we hire a gardener to trim, mow the lawn, and all."

Tim whistled. "Forty-six years. That's a long time to be in one place."

"We've been in this house forty-nine years," Ernie said. "I brought my Bets here as a new bride."

"Yes, he did," she said. "Carried me right over the threshold too!"

"Where are your kids?" Tim asked.

"Scattered here and there, but not far," she said. "I'm on grandmother duty somewhere at least once a week."

"You married, son?" Ernie said.

"No," he replied.

Betsy smiled at him. "But I bet a handsome guy like you has a steady girl."

"Had one, but I kind of messed things up," Tim said.

"Well, you'd be surprised what the words 'I'm sorry' can do," Ernie said. "Always works for me."

"Me too," Betsy said. "I can tell by your expression that she's someone very special. Don't let her go, honey. You'll always regret it if you do."

Tim smiled, wondering how he'd gotten into a discussion like this with clients he barely knew. "That's the advice I've been hearing."

Betsy nodded, offering him, then her husband the plate of brownies. "That's 'cause folks care about you and her. People who care about you want you to be happy."

Tim bit into his brownie. "This is one good brownie."

Betsy beamed. "Old family recipe. They're called blondies. Now, young man, let's talk about your next project for us. I want to commission some furniture for my daughter's new home."

They chatted awhile about Betsy's vision and her daughter's needs, then Tim rose and thanked them for the lemonade and advice. As Ernie handed him an envelope with his check, he said, "Go after this girl, son. My Bets is right. You'll regret it if you don't."

Easy for them to say, Tim thought as he pulled into Buster's Burgers just outside of town. *I would like nothing better than to be with Gail again, but I still stop short when I think of her and what's best for her, Elise Nolan be damned!*

CHAPTER 45

Richard sat by his daughter's bedside, Lucy beside him as Gail's siblings came in and out. Gail was conscious but still had a high fever and drifted in and out of sleep. They had run a series of tests and were waiting for the results.

"What the hell's keeping them?" Richard said. "We've been here for hours!"

Pam put her hand on his shoulder. "Calm down, Dad. They're doing their best. Why don't you and Lucy take a break and get something at the cafeteria?"

"Good idea, sweetheart," Lucy said, patting his hand.

Richard shook his head. "Not leaving her till I get a doctor to talk to me!"

Pam and Lucy exchanged looks, then surrendered to his wishes. Pam pulled up a chair, and Weezie and Rich went to get drinks and snacks for them. Ava arrived shortly after and hugged her father, then Lucy and Pam.

"What is it?" Ava asked.

"They don't know," Pam said. "We're waiting on the bloodwork."

"And if it's much longer, I'm getting a chopper and taking her to Boston," their father said.

Ava's eyes widened, and she gazed from Lucy to Pam. The latter shook her head, indicating that reason and calm had deserted their father.

After what seemed like hours, cups and bags untouched on the tables around them, Gail woke and said, "Listen, gang, I probably have the flu. Why don't you all go home? For that matter, why can't I go home? I'd much prefer my own bed to this uncomfortable contraption."

Wolfie gently smoothed hair back from her feverish brow. "I thought hospital beds were supposed to be super comfortable, sis."

"Not this one. Don't you all have things to do?"

Her father squeezed her hand. "We're doing what we're s'posed to do, pumpkin."

"Dad... Don't call me that," she said groggily, closing her eyes. Irrationally, the one person she wanted here was absent. Her dear loving family surrounded her, but she longed to see Tim.

In the late afternoon, a tall physician in dark blue scrubs appeared. His straight sandy hair was mussed as if he'd just removed a surgical cap and hadn't bothered to tame it down. "Hello, folks, I'm Doctor Leonard."

With a quick glance at Gail, who appeared to be sleeping, Richard jumped up and came to meet the young doctor. "Richard Morgan. Gail is my daughter. What have you learned?"

"Your daughter's lucky she landed here, Mr. Morgan. This is a CDC lab center, so they have the equipment and expertise to identify tick-borne diseases rapidly."

"Tick-borne?" Richard said.

"Yes, your daughter has babesiosis. It's a malaria-like parasitic infection of red blood cells. The team was able to identify the parasite *Babesia microti* in Gail's blood specimen. Symptoms of babesiosis can be mild to life-threatening. Often the symptoms are a high fever, sweats, and nausea, which she has."

"Can you treat it?" Pam asked.

"Of course they can," Richard said, turning to the doctor. "Can't you?"

Dr. Leonard looked from Richard to Pam, then to all the concerned faces in the room. "Yes, we can treat her. There are several protocols, but I would like to use one where we administer clindamycin and quinine. This is the standard for severely ill patients, which your daughter is at present. With your permission, I'd like to start the clindamycin intravenously now."

"Are there side effects?" Pam asked.

"There can be, which is why I'd like to keep her overnight, see how she does. If she tolerates the antibiotic regimen and she responds to the treatment, I see no reason why she can't go home tomorrow with a prescription for both meds."

Lucy stood beside Richard, holding his hand. "What are the side effects we can expect?"

"Probably mild to none, but some patients are nauseous or experience some vomiting. We'll watch her closely. I'd suggest that you all go home and get some sleep."

"I'm staying," Richard said, "but that's good advice. You all go. Lucy, your kids need you, and the rest of you have work to do."

"Not tonight Dad," Rich said. "But this is what I suggest. We'll go and then take shifts. I'll come back and relieve you at midnight."

"Nope, I'm staying. I'll call now and get a recliner delivered."

Pam shook her head at her brother. "Come on, everyone, let's allow them to treat her."

The group stood talking in the hall for a short time, then everyone departed except Lucy. She returned to the room and sat beside her husband, head on his shoulder. The first dose of medicine had been administered, and Gail was asleep.

"What about the kids?" he asked.

"They're fine. They love your guys, and they have a ton of homework. With Callie's food and their stepsisters around, they'll never know I'm gone."

"I love you," he said, kissing her softly. "Some honeymoon, huh?"

"I wouldn't have it any other way."

Richard kissed her forehead. "Just when I thought I couldn't love you more."

"Not as much as I love you," Lucy whispered, looking up just in time to see a smile on Gail's face. Her eyes were closed, but she was definitely smiling.

*****

"Hey, buddy, burgers are here," Tim called, pushing open the barn door.

"Be right out," Coop said, his voice muffled under his metal welding helmet.

A few minutes later, he appeared, red-faced and sweaty, a bottle of water in his hand. "Let's have 'em. I'm starved."

They ate in silence for several minutes. As he tossed his empty burger box into the trash, Coop cleared his throat. "Heard some news when I went down to the Café for coffee."

"Yeah?" Tim gazed over to find his friend's expression serious.

"Thought I'd better let you eat before mentioning it."

"What?" Tim eyed him. "Did they find out something about Izzy?"

Coop shook his head. "Nothing about that. You know the sirens we heard before you left?"

"Yeah?"

"That was Gail."

Tim leapt up. "Gail! Why the hell didn't you say?"

"'Cause I didn't think ten minutes would hurt, and I knew you'd want to run off half-cocked."

"What happened? What's the matter?"

"All I know is that she fell ill, and they took her to the hospital."

"Geez," Tim said, grabbing his phone. First, he punched her number, which went straight to voicemail. Then he tried Richard's. No answer. Finally, he called Dan Fielding.

Ava's husband answered on the first ring. "Hey, Tim, what's up?"

"I'm calling about Gail."

"Yeah, she's in the hospital. Ava and the rest of the family are with her. I'm with our kids."

"What happened? What's wrong?" Tim said.

"As far as I know, they're still waiting on tests. Ava said she'd text of they knew anything."

"Is there anything I can do?" Tim paced up and down the barn, kicking sawdust and wood chips out of his way.

"I'd guess just hold tight and see what they tell us."

"Thanks, Dan, I will. Mind if I call back later?"

"No problem. Call anytime."

Tim clicked off, but continued pacing.

"What's the story?" Coop asked, watching him.

"Gail's sick with something. Must be serious, 'cause they don't know what it is."

"Don't jump to conclusions, buddy."

"I can't just sit here and do nothing."

"Didn't Dan say to call back?"

"Yup."

"Then why not wait a while and call? Then you can make a plan."

"I gotta get out of here," Tim said, grabbing his keys and jacket. "Lock up, okay?"

"Sure thing. Want me to come with you?"

"Nope, I'm all set."

Tim hopped into the truck and drove down Main Street. He had no idea what to do or where to go. After circling the block several times, he headed out to Land's End. When he drove in the long dirt drive, he spied his dad on a tractor headed for the barn. He followed him and parked alongside the barn.

"Hey, son, this is a surprise. Did we know you were coming?"

"Nope."

"What's up?"

"I don't know. Is Mom inside?"

"I imagine so."

Father and son headed up to the house, where they found Faith Miller shelling peas on the back porch. "Hey, guys. I was just thinking about you, honey," she said, looking up at Tim.

"Oh?"

"Helen Winthrop called a while ago and said Lucy told her your girl was taken to Saint Elizabeth's today. Some mysterious virus or fever or something."

Too worried to bother correcting the "your girl" statement, Tim said, "What else did she say?"

"Nothing. Lucy said they didn't know what was wrong except that Gail had a very high fever and had fainted."

"Poor girl," Rex Miller said. "Want something to drink, son?"

Tim shook his head as he began pacing up and down the porch. His parents exchanged looks as they watched him.

Finally, Faith cleared her throat. "Don't take this the wrong way, honey. I mean we always love to see you, but why are you out here anyway?"

"Because I don't know what the hell to do!" Tim said, flopping into one of the porch rockers, head drooping

Rex regarded him for a minute, then said, "Well, what do you want to do?"

"I want to see her," Tim said.

Faith set down the bowl of peas. "Well then, I'll repeat what I just said. Why the heck are you out here instead of at Saint Elizabeth's?"

Tim looked up, staring at her. "Because I have no right to be there."

"Now that's just nuts," Rex said. "You love her. She loves you. Who deserves to be there more than you?"

Confused, Tim looked over at his father. *Have I fallen down the rabbit hole or gone stark raving mad?* "But how did you…?"

Rex laughed. "Son, do we look like we were born yesterday? Now, if you want to go to Saint Elizabeth's, get in your damn truck and go. All they can do is kick you out."

Faith swatted her husband with the dish rag that had been lying in her lap. "Which they won't! I'm sure it will be a great comfort to the Morgans to have you there."

Tim stood and paced for a few more minutes, then said, "Fine, okay. I'll go. Yup, I'm going. I'm going right now."

As his son headed for his truck, Rex looked at his wife. "Hope he doesn't self-destruct before he gets there."

"I hope she's okay, poor girl."

"That too," he said, giving her hand a squeeze.

CHAPTER 46

When Tim reached Saint Elizabeth's, he spied Rich, Pam, and Weezie Morgan walking out of the emergency room door, Ava and Wolfie right behind them. He hopped from the truck and ran to meet them. They quickly related the day's events and the doctor's conclusions.

"They're starting treatment now," Rich said. "Dad and Lucy are staying with her."

"Do you think… I mean, I probably shouldn't be here, but I wondered if I could see her?" Tim asked. He thought he detected a frown on Pam's face.

"Of course you can," Weezie said. "She'd love to see you. She's in 301."

"She's been drifting in and out of consciousness," Pam said. "So she may not know you."

"You're all leaving?"

Rich nodded. "It was getting crowded in there, and they suggested we clear out for the night. You go on up, though. Maybe you can get Dad and Lucy to take a break and walk the halls or get something to eat."

"Thanks, man, I'll sure try," Tim said, saying goodbye and hurrying inside.

When he reached room 301, the door was ajar. Tim peeked in. Gail was sleeping with her father holding her hand and Lucy's head on his shoulder. He stood debating whether to interrupt the tender scene, when a nurse came up behind him. "Are you going in or out?" she asked.

As Tim stepped aside to allow her to pass, Lucy turned and spied him. "Tim, hello, come in." She stood and crossed the room to embrace him.

As Richard came to shake his hand, Tim asked, "How is she?"

"They've just started the antibiotic that should help her to fight it," Lucy said.

"We start the quinine now," the nurse said as she injected a solution into the IV bag.

"She has a tick-borne illness, babee something," Richard said.

"Babesiosis," Lucy said, her arm circling her husband's waist. "It's very treatable, and they expect her to make a full recovery. The next twelve hours will let them know if this protocol works and whether she can tolerate it. They do have other options."

Tim gazed from one to the other. "Is it okay that I'm here? I don't want to intrude."

"Of course it's okay that you're here," Richard said, reaching out to pat his arm. "She's sleeping right now, but you can sit with her, if you like."

"And we can give them a few minutes' privacy, my darling," Lucy said. "I'm starved. How would you feel about taking me to dinner in the cafeteria?"

Richard hesitated, gazed back at his daughter, then said, "Of course. Take good care of her, son."

"Will do, sir," Tim said, as they followed the nurse out, closing the door.

"Hey, sweet girl," Tim whispered, stepping near to the bed and sitting down. She looked impossibly tiny and deathly pale, her beautiful face relaxed in sleep. He took her hand in his, leaning forward to kiss her delicate fingers.

The door opened again, and a tall, skinny physician came in. "Hey," he said. "Don't think I've met you. I'm Dr. Leonard. Skip, actually. You another brother?"

Tim stood and shook his hand. "A friend."

"How's she doing?" Leonard asked.

"I was going to ask you."

"Well, as a friend, I can't really tell you anything, but we're hopeful these meds will make the difference."

"And if they don't?"

"Babesiosis is one of the worst. Patients respond in all different ways. Has she been awake since you've been here?"

"No, but I just arrived five minutes ago," Tim said, watching as the doctor examined Gail. There was a disturbing gravity to his expression and body language.

"She's going to be all right, isn't she?"

Leonard turned to him. "Let's see how she does tonight. If she wakes, please have the nurse buzz me. I'll be in the on-call room all night."

With that, he disappeared, leaving Tim frightened and desperate. He sat back down and took Gail's hand. "Come on, baby. You can fight this. Please. There's so much I want to tell you about what a horse's ass I've been. About how much I love you and can't live without you. Please, sweetie, fight. I'll be right here with you." Gail slept on, and he lowered his head to rest beside her on the bed. *Please, God, let her be all right!*

CHAPTER 47

The sound of scraping startled Tim, and he awoke to see two men moving what appeared to be a double-wide recliner into the darkened room. Richard and Lucy stood supervising them. "This'll be fine, by the window," he said. "Give the kids some space."

Tim hopped up. "Sorry sir… Did you want to sit here?"

"Absolutely not. Why do you think I ordered this king-size recliner? So I can sleep with my gal in comfort. You stay there, unless you want me to order another one of these?"

Despite the gravity of the situation, Tim smiled. "No, thanks, sir. I'm fine here."

As the movers departed, the door swung open and Dr. Leonard appeared. He eyed the recliner, one eyebrow raised. "I'm not even going to ask how you managed that. Has she woken?" he asked, approaching the bed.

"Not while we've been here," Lucy said. "We did step out for dinner." She gazed over at Tim, who shook his head.

"Although, as you saw, I was sleeping on the job."

Leonard examined Gail, squeezed the IV bag, and checked her chart. "Hopefully, this nice long sleep she's having is her way of fighting the infection."

Richard stepped forward. "Is that what you really think, Doc?"

Leonard met his gaze, his eyes soft. "These diseases are idiosyncratic, Mr. Morgan. We don't know a lot about them, and each person's response seems to be different. Let's see how she is by morning, then we'll make further treatment decisions. I'm here all night, and I've asked Gail's friend…"

"Tim," he said.

"I've asked Tim to have the nurse get me if she wakes. You too. Get some rest, folks," he said, nodding to each them as he headed out the door.

Tim looked at the others. "I'd like to stay, if that's okay?"

"Of course," Richard said. "Still think I should order you up a recliner."

"I'm fine, sir, just gonna step out and find a men's room. Then I'll resume my post, unless you want to sit with her?"

"You might want these," Lucy said, handing him a small zippered plastic bag. It contained a toothbrush, toothpaste, comb, razor, and a tiny tube of shaving cream. "I asked them at the nurse's station for three of these."

Tim nodded. "Thanks, that was kind of you."

Lucy hugged him. "She's going to be fine."

He nodded, then hurried out of the room. *If she's not fine, what the hell will I do?*

*****

Tim spent the night at Gail's bedside holding her hand, head and shoulders on the mattress beside her. He was aware of nurses coming and going, but for the most part slept soundly for the first time in several months. He heard not a peep from Lucy and Richard across the room under an enormous eiderdown. At dawn, he was aware of a movement beside him, and Gail squeezed his hand. When he gazed up, her eyes were open and she was smiling.

"Hey, you gave us quite a scare, sweetie," he said, kissing her palm.

"What's going on?"

"You're awake, that's what's going on. How do you feel?" Tim longed to take her in his arms, but resisted, content to gaze into her beautiful hazel eyes, so soft and warm as she looked at him.

"Like I've been hit by a bus. And a bit nauseous, like I might be sick."

Tim reached over and pushed the nurse's call button, then found a small plastic bowl. "Here, if you need it. The nurse'll be here soon."

"It feels like the world is spinning," she said as he smoothed hair from her still-feverish brow.

"You've still got a temp. That's probably why," he said as a nurse came in. Richard and Lucy began to stir.

Tim stepped back. "She says she feels nauseous."

Gail began to vomit into the plastic bowl. "This is perfectly normal with this med," the nurse said. "I've called Dr. Leonard. He should be here shortly."

The next hour was a blur as they ministered to Gail. Leonard ordered ice packs and two nurses to rub her down. The vomiting ceased, but she began to shake uncontrollably. In the midst of this, the doctor turned to them. "Folks, I'm going to suggest that you step out for a bit while we tend to her. I'm pretty sure that's what she'd want."

"I agree," Lucy said, dragging Richard toward the door. "Let's find some coffee, sweetie."

"I'm not leaving her!" Richard said.

"I'll stay," Tim said. "I promise I'll stay back out of the way," he added, directing his words to Leonard. Then he looked back at Richard. "I won't leave her alone, sir. I promise."

"Tim!" came a weak cry from the bed, and Gail reached out with trembling arms.

"Can I?" he said to Leonard. The doctor nodded, and he went to opposite side of the bed, lifting her into his lap as he lay underneath her. "Ice us both," he said as the nurses rolled in a cart loaded with bags of crushed ice.

"Are you sure?" Leonard asked.

"Go ahead," Tim said, arms around Gail, cradling her.

By the time the ice had been exhausted, Gail's fever had broken. She was sweaty and shivering, but more alert. Leonard returned, checked her vitals, and said, "Good, the meds are finally working. I'm going have her shower. Let's see how she does. Why don't you let the nurses take her, and they can find you some dry clothes."

Tim stood, cradling Gail in his arms as he turned to the nurses. "Lead the way. I'll get her there, then you can take over."

CHAPTER 48

The river was glassy as Tim motored out toward the bay. He'd slept for the first time in three days and felt a little better. What he really wanted was to head over to the farmhouse and park himself at Gail's bedside until she was fully recovered, but his pots needed attention. After pulling them all and rebaiting, he had two dozen lobsters in baskets on the deck. He'd discovered a few new poacher traps which he pulled and released the horseshoe crabs. He had just rounded the point headed back to the docks when he spied them, pulling a trapful of crabs. It was the same crappy boat he'd been chasing for months.

Intent on their task they hadn't seen him. Tim gunned the engine and before they turned he was almost upon them. He drew alongside them, "Hey, that's illegal. Release the horseshoes now!" he called.

"Screw you asshole," said a beefy man. In each hand he held a crab by its long pointed tail as the creature bent and squirmed.

Tim pulled out his fisheries badge and held it up. "No, screw you." He grabbed a pen and paper, jotting down the boat's registration number as the crew of three turned away and opened their engine full throttle.

Tim grabbed his cell phone and called the lab. As he watched the poachers disappear around the mouth of the river, he spied a Coast Guard cutter in pursuit. He dialed the lab again and got his aunt. "That was quick," he said.

"They were on patrol a quarter mile away so we got lucky," Grace said.

"Drop in the bucket."

"Yes, but they'll pull their license and registration so that boat, at least, is done for the season."

"I've seen one of those guys before. He's got a bunch of boats. We won't stop him."

"Well you stopped him today nephew. Give yourself a pat on the back. How's your girl doing?"

"Okay as far as I know."

"What's that mean? Haven't you checked in?"

Tim shook his head. *Big families…aunts who think they're my mother.* "I'm in touch, no worries."

"Good cause she's a keeper."

"Bye, Auntie," he said, clicking off.

Truth is, she's right, he thought, punching in the farmhouse number. Lucy answered. "Hi Tim, how are you?"

"Great. Just nailed a boatload of poachers."

"Good for you."

"I didn't want to call her cell and bother her, but I just wanted to call and check on how Gail is doing."

"Much better. She's sleeping now."

"Has it been okay that I've stopped by a couple of times?"

"Absolutely. Any time. We love to see you and I know she does too."

He thanked Gail's stepmother and rang off, heading for the docks.

*****

Three days later, Gail lay on a chaise lounge on the porch, enjoying the morning sun. The medication had done its job, and she was recovering, the antibiotic slowly fighting the debilitating protozoan parasite in her system. She had been home for two days and nights, and, while weak, she was able to attend to her own needs around the house. Her father, Lucy, and her siblings had been waiting on her hand and foot until today, when she had insisted they leave her alone.

Tim had been by, briefly checking in, but despite her family's warmth, he wasn't sure about his place. Gail missed him but was loath to reach out for fear of the crushing hurt that would follow if he withdrew again. She had asked Lucy about Izzy, assuming she might have heard something from Frankie, but for the most part, she was in the dark about that subject.

"Hey, sis," Weezie said, stepping out on the porch. "I'm heading down to the barn. Want to come?"

"Thanks, I'm happy here," Gail said. "This is the first day my head's been clear enough to work." She pointed to her laptop on the table beside her.

"I'd hold off on that as long as possible. Everything's running smoothly, from what I hear. Their biggest issue is figuring out what to call Wolfie. I mean, how lame is that?"

"Not lame at all. That's on my list today, to fiddle with his page. It's a great pic of him. Once we know what to call him, I'm sure Mr. Gorgeous will bring in lots of business."

"*If* we called it Man of the Mountain Winery. He looks like someone from the Maine woods."

"Ha-ha. Have a great day down there. Maybe I'll walk down later."

Weezie headed off, and Gail reached for her laptop just as her phone rang. She saw Tim's name and clicked on. "Good morning."

"Hey, how are you feeling?"

"Better. The antibiotics make me feel like crap, but they seem to be doing their job."

"Sorry I haven't been over much. Didn't want to intrude."

"No worries there," she said.

"Are you getting out? I mean, have you been to town?" he asked.

"No, but I need to go in tomorrow. I'll be fine."

"What about Monday?"

"Open so far, but I'm needing to catch up on a ton of work. Hey Lucy told us you caught the poachers."

"One boatload. Drop in the bucket."

"But still, that must feel good."

"It does, thanks. So…do you think you'd feel up to a boat ride late Monday afternoon? I could grab stuff for a picnic?"

"Sounds perfect," she said. *That is if I don't get seasick and throw up all over you.*

"Okay then. I'll pick you up about five Monday, unless you call and tell me you're not up to it."

"I'll be fine. See you then."

As she rang off, Gail wondered at the invitation. In the hospital, she had had a beautiful dream where Tim had professed his love and told her he couldn't live without her. It was agony to wake up from that.

*****

Monday morning, Tim and Coop were both in the shop when Frankie stopped by. Tim immediately shut off the lathe and went to meet her. She was admiring Coop's handiwork on a table lamp. "I've got to order one of your lamps," she said. "They'd be perfect in my house. Think they'd hold a leaded glass shade?"

"No problem," Coop said, "unless it weighs eighty pounds. Might be good to bring it in when you commission the base. That way I can adjust if we need a heavier bottom."

"Will do," she said.

"Hey, Frankie," Tim said, unable to wait any longer. "Have you got news?"

"Only that there's no news. They haven't given up, but they've kind of hit a dead end. No one's talking, and the people who did it are long gone."

"Sounds to me like they've given up."

Frankie gazed at him, eyes warm. "I think they've given it to the feds. I'm sorry, kiddo. Wish I had better news."

"Time to let it go, buddy," Coop said, exchanging looks with Frankie.

Tim shook his head. "So Izzy was just a throwaway? A piece of trash not worth bothering with?"

"No one's saying that," Frankie said. "I was really impressed with the detectives on the case. They are caring, responsible officers. I'm sure they'd talk with you if it would help." She retrieved a business card from her jeans pocket on which she had written the officers' names and contact information.

"Thanks, Frankie. How much do I owe you?"

"Nothing. Darn Yarner discount."

He came forward to embrace her. "Couldn't have gotten through this without you. I owe you big-time. Anytime you want a piece of furniture, lobsters, or even work done on your house, get in touch. Your money's no good with me. I mean that."

"You take care," she said, winking at Coop as she headed out.

When she closed the door behind her, Coop said, "She's good people, isn't she?"

"The best," Tim answered, returning to the lathe to finish turning the table leg.

After work, Tim drove out to Land's End. His father's truck was gone, but he found his mother in the kitchen. She smiled when he came in. "Hey, honey. Want something to eat?"

"I'm good, Ma. You got it?"

Faith Miller wiped her hands on her apron before going to one of the pantry cupboards and extracting a small green box. "Not gonna tell me what you're doing with this?"

"Nope."

"Well, I've got a pretty good idea," she said. "And I couldn't be happier for you."

"Did you tell Dad?" Tim asked, pocketing the box.

"No. You asked me not to. Besides, he'll love to be surprised when you tell him the good news."

"If there is good news. Might be a while. I'm not getting my hopes up."

"I think you'll be surprised, honey."

"Hope so." Tim leaned over and kissed his mother's cheek. "Gotta go, but I'll be in touch."

"You better!" she called, watching her tall, handsome son depart. Relieved to see him smile, she prayed that everything would go well.

CHAPTER 49

"Come on, sis. I'm taking you to lunch," Pam said. It was a warm sunny morning, not a cloud in the sky. "I was thinking Crab Café. What'd you say?"

Gail looked up from a mountain of paperwork. "I say I'd love it, but I'd like to be back for a short nap after. Tim's coming at five."

"Oh?" Pam's blue eyes sparkled.

"It's just a friendly boat ride."

"Uh-huh."

"Never mind those silly looks. We're friends."

"Says you about the guy who never left your bedside in the hospital."

Gail gazed at her sister, wondering if she dared confide in her. Finally, she said, "I had the weirdest dreams when I was in the hospital. Almost like I was hallucinating. They were so real."

"Good dreams?"

"Some. Must have been the meds they were pumping into me. One dream I…I heard Tim's voice… He was telling me he loved me and that he couldn't live without me."

"Maybe it wasn't a dream?" Pam said, sitting beside her. "The man's crazy about you."

"I doubt it. I also had dreams about three-headed monsters and wolves chasing me."

"Well, we know that didn't happen with Dad, Lucy, and Tim watching over you."

"Exactly. And I doubt Tim would be pouring out confessions of love with Dad and Lucy listening."

Pam shrugged, standing up. "I'm going for a run, then I'll shower and change."

"Great 'cause I have a ton of work to do here," Gail said, returning to her papers.

*****

Shortly after eleven, Gail and Pam headed out. Pam wanted to stop at her rental house to drop off a few boxes. She planned to move in the following week. When they pulled into the driveway, Frankie was heading out. "Morning!" she called.

They met her at her car, a pale blue Volkswagen bug. The seats were covered with denim patchwork. *The last hippie mobile*, Gail thought, greeting her with "Hello, morning. I love your house."

Frankie nodded. "Thanks. It's a work in progress. Are you moving in too?"

"I wish," Pam said. "I've been begging her."

"It'll be nice to have neighbors again," Frankie said. "I'd offer you tea, but I've got an appointment."

"Well, don't let us keep you," Gail said.

"We hear you've been really helpful to Tim with the whole tragic thing with his old friend," Pam said.

Frankie nodded, but said nothing. As she turned to get into her car, Gail said, "Is there any news? Did they find who harmed her?"

"Not yet," Frankie said. "I'm off, but we'll have tea or supper soon, I hope," she said, looking at Pam.

"Thanks Frankie. That'd be great," Pam said.

As the bug disappeared around the corner, Gail said, "What was I thinking, being so nosy? She must be horrified."

"I doubt that very much. Come on. You can sit on the porch while I get the boxes."

"I can help!" Gail said.

"No, you can't! Now go sit, and don't stew."

Ignoring Pam, Gail wandered through the house. On stilts, it sat over the river, as did most of the houses on the water side of Beach Street. Two stories, there was a living room, kitchen, tiny bedroom, and bath on the first floor, and two bedrooms and a bath on the second. The kitchen and baths had been refurbished, and the house was furnished in muted cottage colors with comfortable, well-worn upholstery and eclectic antiques. "This is a very cool place," she said as Gail breezed by with a box of books.

"I love it, and you should move in too. Think what a good night's sleep we'll get with the water lapping underneath us all night."

"Unless it's stormy," Gail said.

"Naysayer. Seriously, sis, think about it. The farmhouse is huge, but there are a lot of people there now with Lucy and the kids."

"It *is* awfully nice here," Gail said, walking out to the porch and sitting on the upholstered swing. "Heaven."

"See what I mean? You ready for lunch? I told Lynn we'd meet her at noon."

*****

"These lobster rolls are to die for," Pam said, waving hers around after taking a bite.

Gail rolled her eyes. "Be careful, or you'll lose some of that precious meat. Lynn, it's so good to see you."

"You too. Thanks for inviting me," Lynn said. Her long dark hair was pulled back, and she wore a flowing white peasant blouse and jeans.

Gus's wife is lovely, Gail thought. *Always the quintessential earth mother.* "We see Gus every day," Gail said, "but not you. How are things? Where's little Sorcha today?"

"My neighbor Ruth has her. I'll miss Ruth when we move out to the farm."

"Can't she travel?" Pam asked, nodding as the waitress approached with a fresh pitcher of iced tea.

Lynn smiled. "I'm sure she can and has already said she'd be happy to sit anytime. It's just so convenient and reassuring to have her and Steve next door. He and Gus have a great time trading stories and sharing gardening tips."

"How's life for *you* in the village?" Gail asked.

"Slowly feeling my way. I'm working part-time for Lucy and Lolly, and your brother says there's a job for me in the winery serving room once they're up and running. That might be really cool. My heart's still with teaching and the schools. I'm sure they'd take me on part-time as an OT, but with three little kids, I'm thinking maybe some adult work might be a nice change."

"I hear you," Pam said. "Not that I'd know. We're now living in a house with two teenagers, so life's been interesting."

"Lucy's kids are great," Lynn said, "and both are wonderful sitters. We've been lucky in that department."

Gail watched her sister and Lynn discussing village life, babysitters, and careers as her mind drifted to her outing with Tim later in the day. She had missed him so much since the hospital, and that frightened her. She had worked so hard on their travels to mend her broken heart and let go, but finding him there, holding her hand, had brought all her feelings back. Pam had said he was crazy in love with her. Gail had no idea if that was close to the truth, but it certainly described her feelings for him. *Crazy in love and in danger of major heartache.*

Lynn gazed from sister to sister. "I think I know what Gail does out at the farm, but what's your position, Pam?"

"Unemployed social worker, but that's about to change. I'm working part-time at the schools and am also sharing an office in town for my private practice."

"Oh, where?" Lynn asked.

"Do you know Elise Nolan? She's above Village Books?"

"I've heard of her. Gus thinks she's terrific."

"Well, we've worked out a schedule to share her space. I work Tuesdays,

Thursdays, and Saturdays, and she's changed up her schedule so she's there Monday, Wednesday, and Friday. It's perfect. We share a calendar, and if the office is free, we can also book on the other's days. At the moment, there's no problem since I have exactly no clients."

"That's wonderful," Lynn said as the waitress, Milly, dropped off the check.

"Our treat," Pam said, grabbing it.

"Shall I do the tip?" Lynn asked.

"Next time," Gail said. "This has been fun."

CHAPTER 50

True to his word, Tim drove in at five and parked beside the farmhouse. Gail was the only one home as Weezie was still down at the stables, Pam had taken another load to her house, and Lucy and Richard had taken the kids out to eat. Gail waved from the porch, where she was waiting, then walked down to meet him.

"Hey," he said, bending to kiss her. "Have you got a jacket or sweatshirt? It's kind of breezy out there now."

"Hold on. I'll be right back."

As she hurried up the steps, Tim watched, her beautiful round ass outlined in faded denim jeans, strawberry blonde hair tied back in a ponytail. *Beautiful!*

Gail returned with a blue polar fleece around her shoulders. She held two baseball caps, one of which she handed to him. "Just got these in." Morgan's Fire was stitched across the moss green canvas with the farm logo—a single flame—in the center.

"Cool."

She smiled, and his heart constricted with an ache that took his breath away. "When we get more in, I'll snag Coop one too."

As they drove through town, he asked about her week. Gail wanted to ask about his but was afraid talk would turn to Izzy and spoil the mood. It was so good to see him, have him near, even if this was just a friendly outing.

The wind had died down by the time they reached the middle of the river, and Tim let the boat drift with the tide. He had stowed a small cooler in the bow from which he now extracted a bottle of sauvignon blanc. Gail knew the wine. It was delicious and pricey. "Can you?" he asked.

"Just a sip would be okay, I guess. They say no alcohol with my heavy-duty antibiotic."

"I have water," he said, eyes full of concern.

"I'll risk a sip," she said.

He poured the wine into plastic cups and handed one to her. "Sorry it isn't crystal."

Gail smiled. "This is just fine. What a beautiful night."

"And how beautiful you are," he said, eyes soft.

"Tim… I want… I want to thank you for coming to the hospital and staying with me. It meant a great deal to me and to my family."

"I wouldn't have wanted to be anywhere else."

Gail blushed, unsure of what to say. *Keep it neutral and light!* "I'm sure there are a million places you needed or wanted to be."

"Gail, I want to tell you again how sorry I am for the night at the apartment. I was all messed up, and what I said didn't come out right."

"Let's not go back," she said, suddenly seized by fear. "I can't. Please."

Tim set down his wine and leaned forward, taking her hand in both of his. "No, we won't go back, I promise. But I hope we can go forward."

Before she knew what was happening, he had slipped to one knee, still holding her hand. From his pocket, he took a small green leather box. Gail's eyes grew big as saucers, and she cried, "Oh!"

Tim grinned. "Let me finish, please. Then you can tell me to jump overboard, get lost, swim with the fishes, whatever you like."

She nodded.

"Gail Morgan, I love you more than I've ever loved anyone in this world. The past months have been agony without you. I cannot imagine a life that doesn't include you at its center. I need to see you, to hold you as much as I need air. I'm asking you to marry me, but I totally understand that you might need time to think about it. And if you can't abide the thought of marrying me, I'm hoping you'll agree to be friends."

Gail set her wine on the deck and squeezed his hands. "Yes!"

Tim breathed out a sigh of relief. "To friends?"

"To everything, you wonderful, clueless man! I will marry you, be your friend, and never leave your side for as long as we both shall live!" Gail leaped into his arms, and they rolled back on the deck.

He turned them to their sides, cradling her. "Are you sure, baby? You don't want to think about it?"

Gail stroked his strong jaw and the weathered, ruddy cheeks that she adored. "Not for a second. I've loved you since the first time I met you at Lucy's Christmas party."

"Aw, baby, I would love to make love to you right now, right here, but we might run aground. Hold that thought."

Tim stood and started the engine, then steered the boat toward a quiet, sheltered inlet. Gail stood behind him, arms around his waist, head resting on his strong back, drinking in the warmth she had missed so much. When he reached the middle of the inlet, he dropped anchor. All that surrounded them were marsh and reeds impenetrable to humans, no houses or footpaths in sight.

Tim turned around, holding her. "Now, my beautiful girl, where were we? Lucy's Christmas party? That long?"

"That long," she said, kissing him deeply. She could already feel his arousal. How she had missed the thrill of anticipation when he held her.

As his hands cupped her breasts, he broke the kiss and grinned down at her. "You looked pretty spectacular that night, as I recall."

"Thank you," she said, a shiver of pleasure rippling through her as his hands slipped under her sweater and found her breasts, teasing and stroking her nipples to rock hardness. "Oh, oh, oh!" she murmured.

Tim trailed kisses down her neck, sucking and licking. "What do you think? Want to stop or take this further?"

Her hands on his fly, Gail said, "What do you think?" She unzipped and released him, her hands stroking his cock as Tim's breathing grew raspy and he groaned.

"Geez, baby, what can we do about those sexy skintight jeans you're wearing?"

"Well, if I can get you out of yours, you can certainly find a way," she said, smiling as he slipped his hands under the front of her jeans, finding her hot and wet.

"Watch me," he said sliding the jeans and her panties off with lightning speed. "Here we go again. Come here, sweet girl."

Tim freed a condom from his pocket, and she took it, gliding it on as her fingers continued to drive him crazy. He lifted her, wrapping her legs around him as he sat back on a cushioned bench. "You ready, babe?"

"Always," she whispered, kissing him as he drew her close and his cock found her moist, hot depths. Gail reared up and came down on him, hard and urgent at first, then slowing down to savor every delicious sensation.

"Do you know how much I've missed this?" he asked, hands gripping her ass as he thrust again and again.

"I think I do." She smiled as all rational thought was obliterated in a blinding fire of sensation.

Afterward, Gail rested limp in his arms. "You know, I had a wonderful dream in the hospital."

He looked up, meeting her soft hazel eyes. "Oh?"

"I dreamed you told me you loved me and couldn't live without me. I think that's what brought me back to the land of the living. Wonderful what strong meds'll do."

"It wasn't meds," he said, kissing her softly. "I said all that, and I meant it."

She gave him a shy smile. "I was hoping you'd say that. Now I have a question."

"Anything, sweetheart."

"Can I please see what you have in that little green box?"

Tim laughed, leaning over to grab the box from the bench. "It was my grandmother's," he said, opening the lid to reveal a diamond ring surrounded by tiny sapphires in an antique setting. "If you don't like it, we can pick out whatever you like. Your dad told me your birthday was in September, so I thought you might like the sapphires."

"I love it," she said as she held out her hand. "It's perfect."

Tim slipped it on, then kissed her hand. "I love you."

"I love you more," she said, arms circling his shoulders. As she shifted slightly, she felt him grow hard inside her. "Hmm... What do you think, fiancé? Have you got anything left?"

"I've always got it left for you, babe, but you're the one with the tick disease. You sure you're okay?"

"Only way I won't be okay is if I don't have crazy, unbridled, mind-blowing sex with you right now!"

The sun set as they found their rhythm and brought each other to the moon once again. In the aftermath of their lovemaking, as they sat cradled in the warmth of each other's arms, the bugs came out. Quickly, they dressed.

"I have food in the cooler," Tim said, "but let's get out of this mosquito bog first. We can eat on the river." He drew her close. "You warm enough?"

"Yes, and I like the plan of getting away from the bugs, but I will be very sorry to say goodbye to you tonight."

"No worries, babe. It won't be for long."

As Gail nibbled a delicious chicken salad wrap, the boat drifted slowly downriver. "So what did you mean when you said 'It won't be for long'?"

"I mean, you can move into the apartment tonight, if you want, and we can get married tomorrow."

She smiled. "You have no idea how appealing that sounds, but as long as I know you love me, maybe we can take a little time with the moving in and marrying? If it's okay with you, I'd like to have a real wedding."

"You're the boss. And besides, my mom would never forgive me if we eloped."

"Does she know about this?" Gail asked, holding up the ring.

Tim smiled, the beautiful secret smile she liked to think of as hers alone. "She gave it to me yesterday, but I didn't tell her what I was going to do with it."

Gail leaned forward and kissed him. "I love you, Tim Miller, and I will love being your wife."

"Ditto." He kissed her deeply, then stood up. "If I don't watch out, we'll ram the dock. Hold that thought, my love."

*****

Please read on for sample chapters of *Pam's Garden*,
book three in the *Morgan's Fire* series!

PAM'S GARDEN

*I am so excited to bring you a sneak preview of **Pam's Garden**, book three in the Morgan's Fire series, which debuts in September of 2019. Pam and Sandy's story is filled with angst, heartache, and, of course, the healing power of love and family. The new and familiar characters of Morgan's Fire continue to live and work in the beautiful New England seaside community of Horseshoe Crab Cove. Obstacles abound for these lovers, from Sandy's lothario ways and angry ex-wife to Pam's impulsive nature and the very real possibility of a broken heart. Please read on and let me know what you think!*

CHAPTER 1

"If you don't have your things out by noon, I'm calling the cops," Sandy Rodriguez said, glaring at the lanky blonde slouched at his kitchen counter.

A struggling artist, Becca had come to the club one night with friends and latched on to him. Sandy had sworn off women after a string of unsuccessful relationships, but Becca had been witty, and she'd made him laugh. They'd gone out to dinner a couple of times, and she became a regular at Sandy's, the music venue he owned north of the village of Horseshoe Crab Cove. Then one day, he came home from work to find that she had moved all her stuff into his house. Though he'd been too tired to deal with things that night, it was now a week later, and he'd had enough.

Becca screwed her face into a pout. "Fine boyfriend you turned out to be."

"I'm not your boyfriend, Becca. Now what's it going to be?"

She pushed back her stool, sloshing coffee on the white marble counter. "Fine. You would call the cops too, wouldn't you?"

Damn straight, he thought, but said nothing, watching as she dragged the bags he'd placed in the front hall out to her car. Murphy, his club manager, had advised him to change the locks, and Sandy had scheduled the locksmith to arrive in an hour. No more hiding a key under the mat either. As he watched her sullen progression, he decided Becca Martin was not as pretty as he'd first thought. *Too pinched and scrawny. More like a swizzle stick than a woman.* Nothing like Pam Morgan, whom he'd seen around town a few times and taken out for one memorable "catch up drink." Not that he was looking. *No more women for you, buddy.*

Becca plopped into her beat-up sedan and started the engine, never once looking back. As she drove out the driveway, she thrust her hand out, middle finger up. *Nice,* he thought, turning to go back in the house. Just as he was about to close the door, he spied a jogger coming up the street. Becca almost ran her down, and the woman had to jump into a thick bush of rosa rugosa at the side of the road to avoid the car. Sandy ran down the steps to assist and was surprised to find Pam Morgan untangling herself from the thorny beach roses.

"Hi, Pam. Sorry," he called. "Are you okay?"

"What's the matter with her?" Pam asked. "Oh, it's you." Sandy Rodriguez was well known to her family from the summer he'd worked for them in Maine when he was a teenager. Fifteen years younger than him, Pam did not recall the summer her ten-year-old sister, Ava, had swooned over their handsome summer employee, but she had certainly swooned the first time she saw him in Horseshoe Crab Cove. The epitome of a Latin lover, the thirty-nine-year-old club owner, with his long, dark hair, coal-black eyes, and body to die for, gave off the kind of smoldering heat that was hard to ignore. He was also divorced, with a string of ex-girlfriends a mile long. They'd had a drink a month earlier, but that was it. And in a perfect world, that would stay it. He had danger written all over him.

Sandy reached out his hand, and she grabbed hold to step back onto the road. Even in her discombobulated state, she experienced a frisson of sensation at his strong, firm grip. Sensation that coursed through her body head to toe. As soon as she regained her balance, she let go, her breath escaping in a *whoosh.*

"I'm really sorry," he said. "My fault. I kind of pissed her off."

Dressed in running shorts and a singlet, she wore her long strawberry-blonde hair tied back in a loose ponytail. *And oh, those legs!* He might have sworn off women, but he hadn't figured on half-naked Pam Morgan jogging down his street. Finally finding his voice, he asked, "Do you live around here?"

"About a mile that way," she said, pointing to the Beach Road. "I just moved into a rental. I love it."

"Oh, which house?" She paused for a second, and he added, "Sorry if that sounded nosy."

"No, more like neighborly," she said. "I'm in the Fergusons', right next to Frankie Brown."

"The hobbit house. Frankie's, I mean. She's one of my mom's good friends."

She smiled again, shielding her eyes from the bright sun. "Both Darn Yarners, I believe?"

He laughed. "There aren't many people in this town who aren't connected to that group in some way. We're an incestuous bunch."

"You're lucky. Lucy, my stepmother, talks about how the Yarners saved her mom's life and how much they did for her and her sisters growing up."

"Ditto to that. Hey, can I offer you a drink? Water or something? Least I can do for almost getting you killed."

Pam hesitated, then said, "Well, a quick drink of water would be welcome, actually. It's hotter than I thought, and I didn't bring my water bottle."

"Great, come on up."

She followed him up the steps of a modern two-story house. The street side was plain, with board and batten siding stained light gray, the front door moss green. "This is a cool place. Did you build it?"

"More like restored or maybe leveled and rebuilt on the footprint. It's a work in progress. Come on in, we can sit on the deck. I'm expecting a contractor soon, so we may get interrupted." He led her through an ultramodern kitchen with light gray cabinets and beautiful marble countertops.

"These are very cool," she said admiring the six stools that appeared to be made out of bleached driftwood.

"Tim Miller's designs. Told him what I wanted, and he built them, but then you know him, don't you?"

Pam nodded. "My sister's fiancé. He's incredibly talented."

"Yup." He pulled a pitcher from the fridge and poured water into two tall glasses. "He's a buddy of mine. Here you go."

His fingers grazed hers as he handed her the glass, and Pam was dismayed to feel her knees wobble. *Get a grip, girl!* she thought, following him out to the deck. "Wow, and I thought we were in heaven on Beach Road!" She gazed, open-mouthed, at his views of the river and bay beyond.

"Yeah, I'm lucky. This is why I bought the place."

As they chatted and watched the river, Pam was aware of her body responding to every cadence of his rich, husky voice. *He's miles too old for you and a lothario to boot,* she thought as he suddenly turned toward the sliders leading into the house.

"That's my contractor. Excuse me."

As he disappeared into the house, Pam came to her senses. Sandy Rodriguez was not only an older man and a playboy, he was also the ex-husband of Lolly LaSalle, her stepmother Lucy's business partner. It had been a very acrimonious divorce, supposedly due to his infidelities, and Lolly still referred to him as "the unmentionable." Gail, her sister, had called him "poison" the one time Pam had remarked upon how gorgeous he was. *Time to go, girl!*

Pam hopped up and went into the house. She placed her empty glass in the farmhouse-style stainless kitchen sink that she suspected had cost more than her week's salary as a social worker. Sandy was in the front hall chatting with the contractor, so she went through. "Mind if I use your bathroom before I head out?" she asked, nodding to the short, bald man with him.

"Sure. I'm in the middle of a renovation of the one down here, so head up the stairs, second door on the right."

She left them and climbed the stairs, passing what appeared to be a child's bedroom. Maisie's, she thought, Sandy's six-year-old daughter with Lolly LaSalle. It was a light, open space, with fuzzy rugs on the floors. A simple four-poster covered in a pastel patchwork quilt and lined with stuffed animals was painted a distressed white matching the dresser and side tables. Bookshelves lined one wall, holding dolls, games, puzzles, and a large collection of picture books. Lolly and

Lucy owned Merlin's Closet, a children's book business, and Pam idly wondered how many of the collection had come from there.

Realizing she'd lingered too long, she hurried in and out of the bathroom also designed with a child in mind. Before heading downstairs, she tiptoed along the hall, peeking into another bedroom that appeared to be used for storage, and then the master suite at the far end of the hall, its floor-to-ceiling windows affording glorious water views. She wanted to go in and peek at his bathroom, which she imagined would be spectacular, but his voice called from below, "Find it okay?" Pam blushed, realizing she'd been caught snooping.

"I couldn't resist peeking into your daughter's room," she said when she rejoined him in the front hall. "It's beautiful. She must love it."

"Not as much as her mom's house at present," he said, "but we keep trying."

"I've got to get going," she said. "Thanks for the water." His smile took her breath away. *No wonder every woman in town is in love with him!*

"My pleasure. Feel free to use this as your pit stop anytime you see my truck in the yard."

"I'll remember that."

"Say hi to your dad for me."

"Will do," she said, slipping out while her legs were still operational. *One more minute staring into those eyes and who knows what might happen?*

As she headed off, Pam noticed the van in the drive, "Cove Locksmiths" printed on its side, and wondered if the reason for its presence was the wild woman who had almost mowed her down.

When she arrived back home, her sister Gail was sitting on her front steps. "Where have you been?" she called. When Pam explained, Gail shook her head. "What did I tell you about him? Poison!"

Despite herself, Pam felt her cheeks redden. "It was a glass of water, not a proposition."

"From what I hear, everything's a proposition with Sandy Rodriguez."

Probably right, Pam thought, leading the way into the house.

CHAPTER 2

"Hey, Murph," Sandy said, finding his manager in the kitchen of the club.

"Hey, boss, where you been?" Murph had been with him since he opened Sandy's ten years earlier. He knew him inside out and had become a close friend. The tall redhead was built like a brick shithouse, which came in handy in his occasional role as club bouncer.

"Following your advice and supervising the locksmith."

"So you managed to evict her?"

He related the incident with Becca and also went on to describe the encounter with Pam Morgan. Finally, he said, "Yup, and Peppy changed all the locks, so I'm good. I've hidden a spare key under the mermaid on the deck," he said, referring to a small cast-iron replica of the Little Mermaid statue in Copenhagen. He had commissioned Coop Merrick, the village blacksmith, to make it for Maisie, who loved the movie and Hans Christian Andersen story.

"Better hope the devious and cunning Ms. Martin doesn't find it."

"Geez, I hope not. I'm hoping she's left town since her friends live up the coast."

Murph studied his boss for a minute. "Think you'll ever find anyone you stick with?"

"Nope."

"You know you're still in love with Lolly."

Sandy gave him a look. "Love her, but not in that way. She's the mother of my child, but we're not compatible beyond that, believe me."

"Well, you're not getting any younger, boss."

"You should talk. How long have you and Sadie been together now?" Ten years younger than his boss, Murph lived with a woman, Sadie Foster, to whom he claimed to be committed. Sandy liked Sadie, but he didn't see a long-term relationship there.

"Two years. We're a work in progress. When she finishes law school, we'll see. I'm guessing the Cove's not quite big enough for her."

"And you won't move with her?"

Murph grinned. "And give up my dream job? No fuckin' way, man."

Sandy laughed. "You're so full of shit, Murphy O'Neill. You know that, don't you?"

"So what about this Pam Morgan? Sounds like you're interested."

"Nice kid. Too young, too normal. She was a toddler when I met her in Maine."

"Sounds like she's grown up now."

"Oh yeah, she's grown up, all right, and gorgeous, but I know her dad. He'd kill me if I dicked her around."

"Hmm… That is a problem," Murph said. "Almost as serious as getting all the beer cooled for tonight. Gotta get cracking. Where are the rest of our lackadaisical staff?"

"Out enjoying this incredible day," Sandy said. "Come on, I'll help you." As he followed Murph into the storeroom, he thought about Pam Morgan's blue eyes and wondered just how angry Richard Morgan, her dad, would be if they dated and Sandy broke his daughter's heart.

*****

"So… Tell me all about Mr. Poison," Gail said as they settled at the Crab Café for lunch.

"There's nothing to tell, and he's not Mr. Poison. He's actually a really nice guy."

"Not according to his ex."

Pam frowned at her sister. "How many people love their exes?"

"Lucy'd have a fit if she knew you guys were dating."

"I barely know the man," Pam said. "We had one catch-up drink a month ago. Period. There's no dating on the horizon."

"Hmm… I would bet big money he'll make a move," Gail said, nodding as the waitress refilled their iced teas and placed their BLTs in front of them.

"Would you stop, please!"

Gail gave her a haughty look. "And what about Ava? She'll be devastated if you start dating her old beau."

"Our dear sister was ten when she had that ridiculous, and embarrassing, crush on him, and she is now *very* happily married."

"First loves last forever!" Gail sang, waving her hands.

"Change of subject, please. What's the latest with you and Heathcliff?" she asked, referring to Tim, Gail's fiancé. "Are you guys moving in together, or do you want to move in with me?"

"I'm staying put for the moment," Gail said. She lived with her sister Weezie, her dad, his new wife Lucy, and her stepmother's two teenagers in the very large and beautiful farmhouse Richard Morgan had built on his farm and winery, Morgan's Fire.

They spent the remainder of the meal talking about the farm and all the projects happening with the wild horse rescue program, the progress of their few thoroughbreds, and the winery at the farm's north end. Finally, Pam said, "Gosh, that was a great sandwich. This place alone is worth the move from Maine. Want dessert?"

Gail set down her napkin. "Always, but I'll skip."

"Me too. Let's settle up. I want to show you something." Pam gestured to the waitress for the check.

The sisters strolled down Mail Street until they reached the curve in the road that led to the north side of the peninsula. "Here we are," Pam said. They stood in front of Village Hardware.

Gail eyed her, puzzled. "This is what you want to show me? What? Have you convinced Dad to bankroll your purchase of the hardware store?"

"I wish. I love these kinds of places, which are, unfortunately, disappearing in the wake of Home Depot, Lowes, and Walmart. No, come on. She's around the back."

Pam led her around to a side door with a small sign that read "Bannister Landscaping."

She knocked, then stepped into a large open space with several tables and all manner of garden equipment. The walls were lined with pegboard where hoes, rakes, shovels, pickaxes, and a number of tools, buckets, gloves, and hats hung. An earthy smell surrounded them as a bespectacled young woman rose from one of the tables and came to greet them.

"Welcome, ladies." The woman, clad in faded jeans and a Village Hardware T-shirt, had wispy shoulder-length blonde hair tied back in a sloppy ponytail and a pencil tucked behind her ear. Although short and wraith thin, she exuded wiry strength in every fiber of her body.

"Gail, this is Kitty Bannister. Kitty, my sister Gail."

The women shook hands as Gail gazed around. "Wow, this is a cool space. I didn't know you were back here."

"My secret warren. My Uncle Tom set it up for me," Kitty said, grinning. Tom "Tack" Walsh owned Village Hardware. A widower, he and his wife, Ellen, had never had children, so village gossip had it that they spoiled all their nieces and nephews. She turned to Pam. "I've got everything laid out. Want to take a look?"

The sisters followed her to one of the tables, where several blueprints lay. "Voila!" Pam said, turning to Gail, then back to the table. "Oh, Kitty, these are beautiful. Just what I envisioned."

Kitty smiled. "Gonna be cool."

Gail gazed at the drawings, a puzzled look on her face. "What is this?"

"Plans for the healing and sensory garden I'm creating," Pam said. "It's been a dream of mine, and now Kitty and Dad are helping to make it a reality."

"At Morgan's Fire?" Gail said.

"No, with Dad's help, I convinced Mavis LaSalle to donate an acre of her property to the village. It's a five-minute walk from here. It's at the very edge of her land, and she's never going to use it, so now it's set to become a community garden. A special kind of community garden where kids and adults can come, have small plots, get their hands dirty. And it'll be handicapped accessible. The raised beds are extra high, which makes it much more accessible to older people who are more comfortable gardening in chairs or for kids in wheelchairs."

"The sensory idea came from that garden we saw in Sussex, remember?" Pam said, referring to their recent trip to England.

"I do," Gail said. "This is amazing."

"And, if all goes well, we break ground next month."

They spent a while talking over the plans with Kitty, then the sisters walked the short distance to the garden site, an open field dotted with shrubs, small trees, and wildflowers. Pam sighed. "Isn't it beautiful?"

"Sure is," Gail said. "I can't believe you pulled this off."

"Mavis signs the papers next week, I think," Pam said. "It's been a dream of mine for so long. Plus it helps me honor Mom." Even after two decades, Laura Morgan's children missed the avid gardener who had also been such a loving mother.

Gail put her arm around her sister. "I'm proud of you, sis. Gonna be so cool. Of course, you know what this means, don't you?"

Pam stared at her. "What?"

"It means that there's no way you can get involved with Mavis' ex-son-in-law. Mavis hates him."

"We're not involved!" Pam said, even as her heart sank. *Gail is right. Any association with Sandy Rodriguez might be the kiss of death for the garden.*

"Well, keep it that way," Gail said. "Let's walk back, and I'll buy you an ice-cream cone to celebrate!"

ABOUT THE AUTHOR

M. Lee Prescott is the author of dozens of works of fiction for adults, young adults, and children, among them *Prepped to Kill*, *Gadfly*, *Lost in Spindle City*, and *Poof!* (Ricky Steele Mysteries), *A Friend of Silence*, *In the Name of Silence*, and *The Silence of Memory* (Roger and Bess Mysteries), *Jigsaw*, and *Song of the Spirit*, and her contemporary romance series, *Morgan's Run*. And now there is *Morgan's Fire* and book two, *Tim's Hands!* Lee is thrilled to be launching three Morgan's Fire titles in 2019. In addition to her fiction, her nonfiction books are published by Heinemann, and she has written numerous articles in the field of literacy education. Lee is a professor of education at a small New England liberal arts college, where she teaches reading and writing pedagogy. Her current research focuses on mindfulness and connections to reading and writing. She regularly teaches abroad, most recently in Singapore.

Lee has lived in southern California (loved those Laguna nights!), Chapel Hill, North Carolina, and various spots in Massachusetts and Rhode Island. Currently, she resides in Massachusetts on a beautiful river, where she canoes, swims, and watches an incredible variety of wildlife pass by. She is the mother of two grown sons and spends lots of time with them, their beautiful wives, and her beloved grandchildren. When not teaching or writing, Lee's passions revolve around family, yoga (Kripalu is a second home), swimming, sharing mindfulness with children and adults, and walking.

Lee loves to hear from readers. Email her at *mleeprescott@gmail.com*, and visit her website to hear the latest and sign up for her newsletters!

Author webpage and Newsletter sign-up:

www.mleeprescott.com

Follow me on BookBub!

www.bookbub.com/search/authors?search=M.+Lee+Prescott

OTHER TITLES BY M. LEE PRESCOTT

Contemporary romances and mysteries by M. Lee Prescott include:

The Ricky Steele Mysteries

Book 1: *Prepped to Kill*

Book 2: *Gadfly*

Book 3: *Lost in Spindle City*

Book 4: *Poof!*

Also, featuring Ricky Steele:

Jigsaw

Roger and Bess Mysteries

Book 1: *A Friend of Silence*

Book 2: *In the Name of Silence*

Book 3: *The Silence of Memory*

Book 4*: Silencing the Pen* (coming in 2019!)

Contemporary Romances

Well-Loved Romances

Widow's Island

Hestor's Way

Morgan's Run Romances

Book 1: *Emma's Dream*

Book 2: *Lang's Return*

Book 3: *Jeb's Promise*

Book 4: *Rose's Choice*

Book 5: *Hope's Wonder*

Book 6: *Ruthie's Love*

Book 7: *Polly's Heart*

Book 8: *Kyle's Journey*

Book 9: *Gus's Home*

Book 10: *A Valley Christmas* (coming in November 2019!)

Morgan's Fire Romances

Book 1: *Lucy's Hearth*

Book 2: *Tim's Hands* (coming July 2019)

Book 3: *Pam's Garden* (coming in fall of 2019!)

Young Adult Historical Romance

Song of the Spirit

Made in United States
North Haven, CT
08 November 2022

26446706R00157